Chrtdes (27)
£3
fiction

Greenland

Arctic Circle

Iceland

York

Frank

N

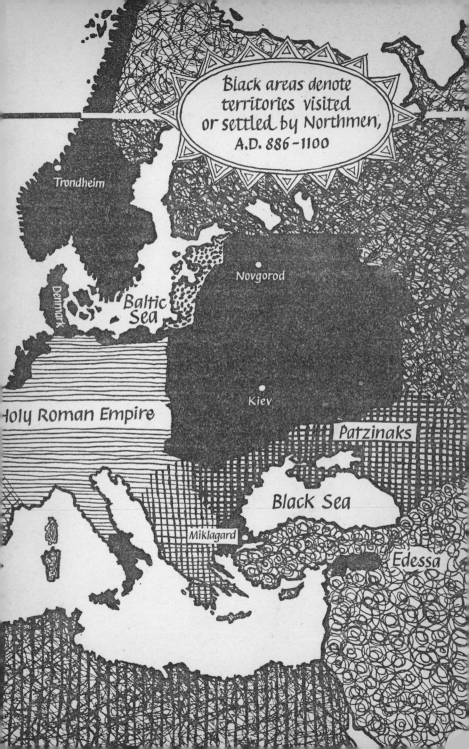

The Last of the Vikings

*Harald Hardrada met his death in 1066,
fighting at Stamford Bridge against King
Harold Godwinson of England. The story
goes that when shown, at his own request, the
fatal arrow that had been taken out of him, he
remarked, 'Yes, the man who made this knew
his trade.'*

*Snorri Sturluson's saga tells us quite a lot
about Harald, and here, Henry Treece,
always at his best when writing about the
Vikings, creates part of Harald's early life
in the form of a novel. Through his stark,
exciting and poetic narrative, the author gives
a brilliant picture of life in those times, and
of Harald himself, who was, in truth, the last
great traditional Viking figure.*

The Last of the Vikings

Henry Treece

Illustrated by Charles Keeping

Beaver Books

First published in 1964 by
Brockhampton Press Limited
Salisbury Road, Leicester, England
This paperback edition published in 1976 by
The Hamlyn Publishing Group Limited
London · New York · Sydney · Toronto
Astronaut House, Feltham, Middlesex, England

© Copyright Text Henry Treece 1964
© Copyright Illustrations Brockhampton Press 1964
ISBN 0 600 35509 8

Printed in England by
Cox & Wyman Limited,
London, Reading and Fakenham
Set in Monotype Garamond
Cover illustration by Neville Dear

Contents

To Anthea

whose opinion I respect

Prologue

Although it was the end of September, the weather up in Yorkshire did not seem to know it, and the sun beat down from a cloudless blue sky for all the world as if it was midsummer. In a broad green meadow beside the river Derwent, a host of men lay under the sunshine, laughing and joking like merry feasters at the end of Lent; or like resting pilgrims on the way to Santiago's distant shrine, forgetting their long journey for a while. Listening to the din they made, a man would hardly know where they came from, for the air was laden with the sounds of Norwegian and Icelandic, of Flemish and French, of Scotch Gaelic and English. There were upwards of two thousand men in the great field, so it is little wonder that the birds were silent and the sunlit sky above them empty. That is, empty save for three carrion crows who circled curiously back and forth, crying discordantly from time to time; and, higher in the upper air, a broad-winged goshawk which hovered at times, almost motionless in the sky, noting everything with his cold sharp eye. Unlike the crows, this hawk was silent, for he was a warrior-bird and knew what manner of men sprawled out below him on the green turf. His watchful eye had told him that this was no crowd of pilgrims, for he had noted the swords and axes, the shields and mail coats, the helmets and javelins that lay everywhere beside the men, on the trampled turf, cast down because of the sun's warmth.

And especially the hawk noticed a broad banner that lay spread over a hillock to keep its white silk unwrinkled, for on this banner was pictured another great bird, the black raven with its wings outspread, Odin's bird.

Close to the raven-banner, three score men sat in a ring laughing, and in their midst, a giant with flax-yellow hair and beard, merrier than the rest. The hawk came lower to look at this man, for he seemed to be three heads taller than all about him, though they were not small men either.

But suddenly the giant turned back his head and with a stiff arm pointed upwards. 'Away with you, goshawk,' he called in a hard voice, 'today's business is for men, not birds. We'll send for you if we need you.'

The men in the circle laughed at this and one of them even took a leather sling and sent a round pebble whistling up towards the bird. The goshawk did not stay to be insulted further, but wheeled with a flick of his broad pinions and rode the warm waves of air towards the west, setting his course for the oakwoods that stood above York.

Down below, the giant laughed and said to the slinger, 'Why, man Ljot, you are almost as good a hand with the sling as you are with the axe.'

'So I should be, King Harald,' said black-bearded Ljot, wrapping his sling up carefully and tucking it into his calf-skin pouch, 'I spent my boyhood learning to cast a stone, up in Orkney, at my father's steading. It was the only way to keep the wild-cat from harrying the new-born lambs. A man can't catch a wild-cat with an axe, you know, Hardrada.'

The giant called Hardrada stared at Ljot, his short flaxen beard jutting out and his thick moustaches hanging down on either side of it. For a moment, his scarred nut-brown face looked harsh. The light blue eyes which gazed out of it, one eyebrow set higher than the other, seemed as cold as northern icebergs. He said, 'Do you think I could catch a wild-cat with an axe, fellow?'

Ljot shrugged his shoulders and grinned. 'Well,' he said, 'you are brisker than most men in the world, as well as being bigger. You have caught many a Turk unawares, and that takes some doing! Besides, you have the blessing of God on you, since you once helped to build the Church in Jerusalem, over the grave of Jesus Christ, when you were soldiering for the Emperor of the Greeks. Yes, on second thoughts, you might outwit a wild-cat.'

The face of Harald Hardrada relaxed into a smile, though such a fierce smile that it was harder to bear than most men's scowling, and he said, 'You did not mention that I am King of Norway. Does that not count?'

Black-bearded Ljot plucked a grass-stem and began to chew it, though he still looked from under his eyelids at the Norse King. 'Aye,' he said casually at last, 'that does count, a little, Harald. But it would count even more if you were King of England as well: then, the wild-cats would run for their lives only to see your shadow on the hillside.'

Harald Hardrada, King of Norway, frowned again and seemed to forget Ljot altogether. Between his clenched white teeth, he said, almost to himself, 'That day has come. That is why we are here. Before this hot sun sets, if God wills it, and my raven-banner, *Landwaster*, has not lost its magic, I *shall* have a second crown to wear.'

Ljot stopped chewing the grass-stalk and said, daringly, 'You will have to share it with Earl Tostig of Northumbria there, since he fetched you over the sea to kill his brother, the English king. Perhaps you could wear the crown turn and turn about: you on Monday, Tostig on Tuesday, then you again on Wednesday. Yes, certainly Wednesday, since that is Odin's day . . .'

But Harald Hardrada did not answer him. Instead, he called across to the next hillock, where a group of English carles stood, leaning on their spears, and talking to a grizzled man who wore a scarlet tunic of fine silk and swung a gilded helmet carelessly on his thick forefinger.

'Hey, Tostig,' cried King Harald, 'which days do you want to wear the crown when we take it from your brother?'

Earl Tostig stopped talking to his spearmen and turned towards the lounging Norse king. 'I have no preferences, my lord,' he said, smiling strangely, 'as long as we can get our hands on it.'

A tall spearman standing next to the earl said under his

breath, 'When we have the crown safely in our grip, it will be a lucky Norseman who ever sees it, much less wears it, at all!'

But Earl Tostig did not seem to hear these words; he only smiled again, with a quick twitch of the lips that spread upwards towards his eyelids.

King Harald of Norway turned away from him, as though he had forgotten him all at once, and said to Ljot again, 'I wonder if you would be good enough to hoist my banner, *Landwaster*, on the hilltop here? I would like to see it flapping in the English breezes. The banner-bearer, old Fridrek, will help you: he has hoisted it many times, and knows how to manage it when the wind gets into the cloth.'

Ljot rose to his feet and said, 'I have sailed from Orkney to Iceland, and back, in autumn gales, two score of times; and each time I have hoisted the sail of my own longship. A man who can hoist a sail single-handed needs no help in hoisting a mere banner.'

King Harald's face became hard at this. His hands were clasped together and when he heard Ljot's words, he clenched his fingers so tightly together that the knuckles cracked. He said, 'After such boasting, you had better hoist my banner well, friend Ljot. I am not short of Orkneymen, remember, but there is only one *Landwaster*.'

Many men, sitting in that ring, wished that Ljot had not been so outspoken and that Harald had not answered him so hotly. Before a battle, it ill becomes any man, king or carle, to speak such words as may be heard elsewhere and remembered, if the luck falls on the other side of the fence.

And now the luck seemed to fall strangely, for as Ljot grasped the tall ash-pole, a sudden gust of wind came from nowhere and wrenched at the heavy silken cloth, bellying it out like a sail so that no three men could have held it, much less driven the iron point into the ground.

Landwaster crashed back to the turf, its long folds whirling about Ljot and dragging him down with it. And though he looked a foolish enough figure on the ground, with his legs kicking out, no one in the ring laughed, or even whispered. The silence that lay upon them all was much heavier than lead. Even the wind stopped blowing.

As for King Harald, his eyes and face had become stone, or iron, or ice. He only said, 'You shall have your chance before this day is out, to prove that you mean well by me.' But these words, though simple ones, were said in such a way that no man who was there did not feel the hairs rise upon his head and neck, as stiff as wire.

Then, all at once, a man in Earl Tostig's company pointed towards the west and shouted, 'Look! Look! The English king is coming to bring us his crown in person!'

All men gazed at the cloud of dust which rose on the road beyond the meadow. King Harald, who was sharper-eyed than other men, said, 'His force outnumbers ours, and will be here before we can put on our armour and make ready for them.'

Then he called across to Earl Tostig, 'Is that small man on the black horse at the front your brother, then? The one with the golden helmet?'

Earl Tostig answered sharply, 'My brother is the one on the black horse, but I have yet to hear anyone call him small to his face.'

The King of Norway smiled gently and said, 'You shall have that pleasure before long, Tostig Godwinson.'

Then he stood up among his Northmen and forgot all else except the battle that was coming. In a loud voice, he commanded his host to cross the single bridge that spanned the river Derwent and to take up their positions on the far side, forming a great shield-ring about *Landwaster*.

Ljot of Orkney began to move away with the others, but King Harald suddenly called him back. 'Your place is not in the far field, hoister of sails and banners,' he said grimly. 'I need you for a more special task.'

Ljot gazed back into the king's cold eyes. 'I am your dog, master,' he said without blinking.

For an instant, Harald Hardrada almost smiled at him: but then he recollected himself and said, 'Yes, you are my dog, and a good dog guards his master's door. I have no door in England at the moment, but I have a bridge; and that you shall guard with your axe, to see that this English king does not pass over the river until we are all armed and ready for him on the other side.'

Ljot slapped his axe-blade and nodded. 'I shall see that you have enough time, Harald,' he said calmly. 'For your part, see that old man Fridrek makes a better job of hoisting *Landwaster* than I did!'

King Harald said, 'He will, fellow. He has not sailed to Iceland twenty times, but he has stood in twenty battles, which amounts to much the same thing. Now, good luck sit on your axe-edge. And, wherever you are going, I wish you a good journey.'

Ljot called at the king's back, 'I shall travel merrily, Harald, which is more than will be said for the Englishmen who set foot on the bridge.'

Then, as the Northmen crossed over, Ljot dragged on his mail shirt and stood waiting, leaning on the bridge and whistling, and occasionally swinging his long axe like a scytheman cutting corn, delighting in the hiss the keen blade made, going through the air.

In his shield-ring, on the far meadow, with great

Landwaster flapping behind him, King Harald of Norway buckled on his own mail shirt. It was very long and reached down to the lower leg. When the king wore it, the Norse carles called him 'Emma' behind his back, because the skirts were so long. In his own sharp way, Harald had got to know of this and now called his ring-shirt by the same name, gritting his teeth gently and sweeping his pale eyes over the carles' faces like a light whip-lash.

'On, Emma, on!' he grunted that hot day. 'Let us have no woman's treachery about you. Keep the arrows out, that is all I ask.'

As he spoke, two strange things happened. First, an angry cry went up from the tight-packed Norse carles in the foremost ranks. 'Ljot is down!' one said. 'Now the English are coming over the bridge.'

Harald was busy with a throat-buckle and, not looking up, asked, 'How did he fare?'

A burnt-faced Icelander called back above his shield, 'He took the heads of three before one went under the planks and poked a spear up into him, the English dogs!'

Harald finished fastening the buckle, then nodded and said, 'When I am their king, I shall have a word or two to say to the captain who ordered such a death, and he will have but short time to answer me.'

As he spoke, he knew that he should not have tempted his fates so, for suddenly a tearing gust of wind came from nowhere and almost flung *Landwaster* down again on the hillock. Fridrek held on to the great ash-pole as though he was wrestling with a troll in the darkness; but it was all he could do to keep the banner upright. And while he struggled, a raven came down over the King of Norway and cried out so furiously in its cracked voice, like a scolding old crone, that all the carles were silent with foreboding. Harald pretended to pick up a stone from the ground and made the action of throwing it. The bird flapped away on its ragged black wings.

The King of Norway laughed and said, 'See, that messenger talks much – but knows nothing!'

Then the second strange thing happened.

There was a marshal in the King's Host, named Styrkar, a tall and gallant man, ever first in the blow-swapping, who carried scars from Sicily and Jerusalem across his face. In all their time together, the king asked Styrkar's advice on battle-affairs more than he did of any other man, for this marshal knew more about war than any five living kings, having spent half his days on battlefields. Styrkar's mother came from Gritriver, near Hlidarend, in Iceland, and claimed to be a kinswoman of Gunnar Hamundarson, which made the marshal of heroic blood. His father was Gizur of Bergen who took a longship to Dublin before his sixteenth birthday and brought it back safely through winter storms, down to the gunwales in water, being so laden with Irish gold that the oarsmen could not even sit down to row, much less lie down to sleep.

So this Styrkar was of the finest birth on both sides, and any king might be glad to ask his counsel. Just now, he was setting the shield-ring, with spearmen in the first ranks to keep the English horses off; then shield-men with their bucklers rim to rim; and, nearest the king and banner, bowmen who could send their arrow-hail over the heads of all in front.

King Harald Hardrada called out to Styrkar the Marshal, 'From where you are, friend, how does it look? Shall we have these English on their backs and knees in time for dinner, do you think?'

In the bright sunlight, Styrkar glanced up at the king with a wet red face, and his lips moved in answer. But the King of Norway stood aghast to hear his words, for his voice had changed so much. In the shuffling and clattering of battle-dawn, it was not Styrkar's high voice that seemed to speak, but the deep voice of Harald's brother, King Olaf. Yet Olaf the Saint had been dead for thirty-six years.

The voice said, 'It ill becomes a man, though he be a king, to weave the future's web with boastful words. No man should speak of dinner till the sword is put away and the cup is at his lips. Here, close by York and beside this river called the Derwent, you should remember other words I spoke to you once when you lay asleep in a burned ship on the plains above Kiev. But, more than that, you should remember Stiklestad, above Trondheim, when we thought we had the beating of Swein of Denmark. Do you remember Stiklestad, Brother Harald?'

The King of Norway nodded and rubbed his eyes as though they were full of sleep and he was trying to be rid of it. None of the carles seemed to notice this, or to hear dead Olaf's voice. It was more like a dream than anything else, and only Harald was in this dream. He gazed upwards, under the flapping banner, and said aloud, 'Aye, Olaf, I remember Stiklestad. It was the first battle I was ever in, and I was only a lad. I *should* remember it – enough happened that day to stay with me all my life. I have good cause to remember it, Olaf. Yes, every second of it, every blow of it!'

Chapter One

The Spears of Stiklestad

At Stiklestad six spears came at Harald, swift as snakes, rattling against each other, ash against ash, in haste to end him. He stumbled on the churned-up turf and fell, the spear-shafts criss-crossing over him like the roof-beams of a house, their iron points in the ground on either side of his body.

'Olaf! Brother Olaf!' he shouted, swinging his round shield sideways and flailing out as well as he could with his sword. 'To the rescue, Olaf, I am down!' His young voice echoed among the rocks, high and shrill.

He heard the rebel-peasants laughing above him, and one of them saying, 'You can cry out for the King, wolf-cub, but he's too busy to help you now!'

Suddenly Harald Sigurdson felt a great fury come over him, and rejoiced when his shield-rim cracked hard against the man's shin-bone, sending him skipping away and groaning.

Then the spear-points came out of the ground with a sucking noise, and Harald knew that soon they would be thrusting at him again, but more carefully now, having missed the first time.

In the little grace allowed him, he rose to his knees and

swept out widely, like a man scything grass. He felt the edge of his sword, *Legbiter*, shock against something, almost twisting from his grasp, and he heard a man shout in pain. Then he just had time to get the broad shield over his head before the iron-points rattled on it furiously again.

He was about to take air into his lungs and call for Olaf once more, when there was a great thudding of feet and a rushing of air, and Harald found himself being lifted high, and being swept away, as though a whirlwind had clenched about his body to carry him up to Valhalla. As he struggled for a moment, he saw that his brother, Olaf of Norway, was close beside him, laughing and red-faced, scything with his long sword, and knocking men away from him as a lion would shake off dogs.

'Courage, brother!' the King was calling. 'We have got you now. We'll teach these carrion crows what it is like to fight with princes.'

Then Olaf's men had set Harald on his feet again, where the ground was more even and there were fewer enemies.

Olaf called back over his shoulder, 'Keep at it, little gamecock. I go to look for our enemy, the Danish king!'

Harald saw his half-brother plunging away like a giant among the brambles, his feet sinking into the sandy soil as he went, and his great cloak flying. Olaf was a fine man, a head taller than most in Norway, his hair almost as white as flax, his shoulders as broad as a barn-door.

'Let me come with you, brother!' the boy called.

But an old warrior dragged at his mail-shirt and said hoarsely in his ear, 'Hold the hill, Harald! You can serve him best here. Why do you think he has brought you to this place?'

Harald looked back at the old man, a bitter answer forming on his lips; but then he saw the smile on the wrinkled, battle-scarred face, and the great slashes in the man's mail-shirt, where his leather tunic showed through. And he said breathlessly, 'Yours is good counsel, Earl Rognvald. I thank you for reminding me of my duty.'

The Earl pulled Harald to one side, so that their house-carles could get round them in a shield-ring. Then he said, 'My own sons were like you, lad, rough unbroken stallions, before they fell under the Danish axe. At fifteen, you are a day too young for such an end. Keep with me, and we shall put an end to these rebel-peasants and their Danish allies, if God will only smile on us a while.'

Harald wiped the streaming sweat from his forehead and said, 'If He does, then one day, when the crown comes to me, Rognvald, I will build a great church for Him, down there at Trondheim. I call you to witness my promise.'

Earl Rognvald nodded and smiled. 'Aye, aye, lad,' he answered, 'I hear you, and I'll keep you to it, when the time comes. Now pull your helmet well down and tighten your throat-mail. Never leave the buckles unfastened. The arrows are flying, and it would be a bad bargain for Olaf to drag you away from the spears to lose you a minute later to the arrows.'

It was starting to rain, on the hill above the dark fiord, and the clouds were sweeping in, low and grey, from the sea, bringing with them hosts of white sea-birds which squawked harshly as they wheeled above the fighting men, as though mocking them.

From time to time arrows whistled out of the miserable sky and smacked viciously into the ground, sinking a hand's breadth before they stood, quivering, where they stuck.

Earl Rognvald called out for the carles to kneel and hold their bucklers above their heads for a while, until the arrow-flights had died off.

One great warrior shouted back, enjoying his taunt, 'What are our helmets for, Rognvald?'

The Old Earl smiled bleakly at him and answered, 'Yours is of no use at all, Thorleif. Your skull itself is thick enough to turn any arrow I have seen; but I am thinking of your comrades, whose heads are less solid.'

The men all laughed at this and raised their shields as the Earl had said. Even Thorleif joined in the laughter, for it would have been unmanly not to take a joke against himself.

It was then that a tight-packed company of peasant Bonders came rushing from behind a clump of dark pine trees, and halting, shouted, 'Death to Olaf! We will have Swein of Denmark for our master, or none at all.'

Earl Rognvald poised his throwing-spear and answered them, 'You will have what you get, you treacherous dogs. And you can have this spear for a start!'

The long shaft whistled through the air towards the Bonder leader, who was running some paces ahead of his band. He was a black-haired man with the sharp eyes of a wolf, and so he saw the Earl's spear coming. No man could deny him courage, for he laughed even as the weapon plunged at him; then, in the last moment, leapt aside so that it only went through the skirt of his tunic.

'There are better spearmen than you, Rognvald,' he called.

But the Earl answered wryly, 'Look behind you, fellow, and see what it did to your brother.'

Then the Bonders were upon them, striking out with billhooks and scythe-blades, as well as with their long-hafted wood-axes. Some of these men felt the blood of battle beating so hard in their hearts that they flung themselves at the spearhedge and tried to leap the points. But Harald's house-carles were old hands at this game. Many of them had faced even the fierce Moors of Andalusia in their time. Only one of the

24

Bonders broke through towards the banner, and this one Harald cut down when he was but a yard away. It was the black-haired leader who had been so nimble and mocking a minute before.

Earl Rognvald spared him a glance and said, 'So, you see, lad, it ill becomes a cock to crow too loudly. Another fox may be waiting round the next corner of the barn.'

It was a hard tussle while it lasted. Some of the Bonders were so quick-sighted that they even caught the spears hurled at them, and returned them at the sender while he was still bent over from the cast. But the house-carles were even brisker; seeing the peasant axes sweeping out, they jumped over them like dancers; at other times, they straddled thrusting spears, like men mounting a war-mad stallion. And always they gave better than they got, using the edge and the horn of the war-axe to bring down their foemen.

There was one old carle, who had been viking every summer for forty years, and knew the world, from Iceland to Jerusalem, like the back of his horny hand. He knew every harbour, and every coastal village where there was a church with a gold cup in it, from Bergen to Antioch. His name was Sigvat and he had lost eight sons on the seas. This made him careless of his own life, but much feared by his enemies.

This day six Bonders came at him, seeing that he was grey-haired and thin-legged, thinking to have him down in a moment. But old Sigvat was not to be taken so lightly. He looked back at Harald and whispered, 'Watch this trick, Sigurdson. If I can bring it off, then at least you will have learned something today.'

Then, with a high shout, he flung away his shield, as though he did not need its protection any longer, and made for the smallest of the Bonders, who was some paces away from his fellows. As the man quailed, taken by surprise,

Sigvat dealt him a shoulder-blow, which toppled him among his mates; then, springing sideways, the old viking began to run outside the shield-ring. So, gaining a few yards start, and stringing his foemen out, Sigvat laid five of them low, some with knee-blows, some with thigh-blows, and one even with a stroke made over his shoulder as he went. The sixth Bonder gave up the chase and setting himself to take careful aim, reached Sigvat in the back with a short javelin as his mail-shirt swung upwards in the exertion of running.

Harald was close to tears to witness such a sad end; but Earl Rognvald struck him across the face, just hard enough to bring his mind back to the matter in hand, and said, 'Sigvat is laughing, where he is. Why should a mere boy weep? You should be sharing Sigvat's triumph, my friend, not moping like a woman.'

By now the shield-ring was less than it had been before, and though the Bonders were broken, there were still Danes to reckon with. Rognvald said, 'Let us shift higher up the hill, then they will find us harder to get at. And maybe King Olaf will see us when he has finished his own foraging and will come up to help us.'

Those who were left of the house-carles obeyed the old Earl, and they were formed in a small ring once more just as the Danishmen came out of the wood with their spears.

This was not like the peasants' attack. The Danes ran tight-packed as herrings in a tub, their spears as close-set as a farmyard fence, so that not even a piglet could squeeze between them. Earl Rognvald drew in his breath and said, 'It will be a lucky man whose hair is not smoothed by this comb. See that you do as I do, Harald, and let us have no more swapping blow for blow until the spears have passed. Stand behind me and watch.'

Harald's eyes were everywhere at that moment. He saw

his carles valiantly trying to hack the iron-heads from the Dane spears as the push was made; he even saw the captain of the carles go up into the air on one point, still angrily trying to reach its holder with his long axe.

Then he saw the carles break and Danish spears coming in a line at him. 'Down on your knees, you fool!' shouted Earl Rognvald, forgetting himself at such a moment.

Scrambling like weasels, the two slid under the spear-points on hands and knees, and then the Earl called out again, 'Strike at their legs. They cannot get at you now, if they keep their formation. Their points have already passed us.'

So, being jostled here and there, kicked and buffeted in the half-darkness, Harald and the Earl struck out to left and right, all the time shuffling on over the tussocky grass, their mouths and eyes filled with the sand that furious Danish feet kicked up.

And at last they were clear, outside the spear charge, with the grey sky and the white sea-birds over them once more, and the Danes still pushing on away from them towards the banner in the broken shield-ring.

The Earl dragged Harald to his feet. 'Come,' he gasped, 'we have been fortunate. It would ill become us to throw our luck back in God's face.'

He set off at a run, round a clump of hawthorn-trees, heading for the brow of the hill, so that they could drop behind it out of sight until their surviving men could join them to make another stand.

And so they both lay behind a boulder, fighting for breath, thankful for the lull in the war-play, when down below them they heard a loud mocking voice which said, 'Are you two fellows weary of the game, then? I thought you Norwegians worked a longer day than this. Come down and let me see you.'

Harald turned his head slowly and saw, twenty paces below, a big man sitting by a stream, his shirt open and his helmet on the grass beside him, as though he was enjoying the sunshine. He was eating a piece of bread and in his other hand he held a horn ale-cup. On either side of him stood armed men with their bows drawn and their sharp arrows pointing up the hill towards the boulder which had sheltered Harald and the Earl.

Rognvald placed his sword on the ground beside him and said, 'Out of the cooking-pot into the fire, lad. I thought our luck was too good to last. We have run right into the mouth of King Swein, like a hare into a wolf's jaws. And it is his dinner-time!'

The Danish king stood up, his food in his hand, as though this was no battle encounter, and called, 'Must I ask twice? Come down, I say. It would be a bad end to my meal if I had to have these good bowmen skewer you before I had finished my bread and ale.'

Rognvald stood then, grasping his sword by the point-end and letting the ivory handle hang down.

'Come, prince,' he said quietly, 'we must face this out, though we have no stomach for it.'

So, at last, they went down the hill and stood before King Swein of Denmark. Harald noted his thick arms and legs and the fineness of his armour, each black iron scale of which was inlaid with silver in the shape of a dragon. But most of all, he noted the Dane-King's face, as brown and wrinkled as well-used Cordovan leather, with a stiff black beard, tinged here and there with grey, and growing right up his cheeks almost to the eyes. And the eyes themselves, light and grey and dancing, like those of a baresark.

'Well,' said the King, 'so now you have looked me over, like a farmer at a market, and what do you think?'

Harald said, 'I think you are the best-looking man I have ever seen, apart from my brother, Olaf. But I think that you are a bad man, for all your warrior face, and it would do my heart good to put an end to you.'

The Dane laughed, his head thrown back, and then he held out his ale-cup to the boy. 'Words break no bones,' he answered, 'and I like a young dog that's not afraid to bark when he meets with a wolf. Drink, my friend, you look thirsty. It would ill become a King to refuse ale to a prince at a time like this.'

At first Harald could not bring himself to take the cup, though his mouth was parched and his tongue as dry as an old piece of oak.

Swein laughed again. 'Come lad, take it,' he said. 'There's no salt in this ale. It will not bind you to be my friend.'

So, at last, Harald drank and then passed the cup to Earl Rognvald. Swein nodded, smiling, and waved to his men to stand a little farther off. Then, pointing towards the flat stone, he said, 'Now let us sit down and talk of serious things.'

Harald flared up and said, 'There is no thing I wish to talk of with a Dane, save his death.' But old Earl Rognvald took his arm and drew him down on to the rock. And then King Swein said between closed teeth, 'Now you have barked enough, young dog, and we know your courage. But do not tempt the wolf too far. His temper is a short one, and it may be in his mind that you, not he, shall die.'

Earl Rognvald said, 'The lad speaks honestly, Swein, he is no thrall or byre-slave. He is to be a king one day, and kings speak their mind, as you know. He should not be harmed for that.'

The Dane smiled, though his smiling was worse than his frowning. And he said, 'Not every egg becomes an eagle. It may fall from the nest and be smashed before it is hatched. Or a man may carry it away and give it to his children so that they can say they have blown an eagle's egg. There is nothing certain in this life, as you must know, old man, for you have seen your family perish when you thought they would grow to be a fine brood of young warriors.'

For a while, both the Earl and Harald glowered at the Dane as though they might leap up and try to kill him, in spite of all his bowmen who ringed them round. But Swein disregarded their looks and, half-shutting his eyes, looked above them towards the hilltop.

'You hate me because I have come with my ships and my swords into your country,' he said. 'But you are wise enough to understand, surely, that I come because your Bonders, your hard-working farmers, are weary of your rule – weary of paying their heavy taxes, weary of bowing down to a harsh king.'

Harald cried out, 'Olaf is no harsh king. He takes his dues, no more. And even if he were what you say, that gives you no right to come here. A farmer does not break into his neighbour's land because that neighbour sows a different crop from himself. A shepherd does not lead away his neighbour's flock because the silly sheep call out to him.'

At first it seemed that King Swein would jump up and strike the lad: but suddenly he laughed and said, 'They told me you were a sharp young fellow, but they did not tell me you were half a priest and half a lawyer already! Oh, lad, it is a waste of a good life for you to go on living in this rainy desert. Forget Olaf, and come back with me to Hedeby and sit on a stool beside my throne. I'll see that you get the crown you want, one day, if you are a good lad and mind your manners.'

Now a great madness came over Harald. His heart beat like a smith's hammer, and the grey clouds came down right over his eyes. He leapt up, though Earl Rognvald tried to stop him, and plunged at the Danish king.

But Swein was stronger and quicker than most men. Harald, in his wildness, felt a hard blow at the side of his head, then he was sprawling at the king's feet, and, high above him, Swein was standing with his sword drawn and flecks of spittle all over his harsh beard.

Yet, even so, Harald's anger had not left him. Snatching out, he grasped the king's ankle and sank his teeth into it, hoping to gain some revenge, however small, against this man who spoke so slightingly of Olaf.

With a sudden hard movement, King Swein kicked him away, and what might have happened then, no man knows; but all at once the world seemed to fall apart. There came a loud shouting from the hilltop, and then men stood dark on the skyline, with their spears bristling and the wild sea-birds swirling about them. For a moment, Harald on the ground thought that it was Olaf and his companions, come to save him. But then he heard Swein's high shout of triumph, answered even more wildly from the hillside: and when he looked more closely, he saw that these men also were Danes, and that they carried with them a great man, whose arms and legs hung down limply, and whose swinging head was white.

Then Harald knew who it was. He knew the tattered banner, with its red ground and its spread-winged raven. And, beside it, he saw other men carrying Olaf's high-crested helmet and his shield garnished with plates of copper and ivory.

Tears spurted from his eyes. His voice went and left him dumb, although he tried with all his power to shout out for vengeance.

Then his head whirled so much that he did not know what

was happening to him. He only felt two strong hands on his shoulders, dragging him up to his feet. And when any sense at all came back to him, he was running beside Earl Rognvald, with arrows slapping into the turf all about him, towards a wood.

'Faster! Faster!' the Earl was crying. 'We may still get clear, while they are rejoicing over the body of Olaf.'

Harald wanted to stop then, and weep again: or to turn back and do his best, against the arrow-hail, to get vengeance for his dead brother. But Earl Rognvald took him by the hair and dragged him on.

'Run! You donkey!' he was shouting. 'There will be time for Dane-killing later. You owe it to Olaf to come clear out of this. So run!'

And when their hearts were almost bursting, and their legs too weak to carry them much farther, the two broke through the spiky brambles and so into a dark pinewood, where the tree-trunks stood, grey and green and solemn, like the pillars of a church, and the thick carpet of ancient pine-needles muffled all sounds their feet made.

'Into this bush,' gasped Earl Rognvald. 'Draw the leaves about you and lie still. They will be coming for us before long, you can depend on that!'

So, they lay, every gasp as painful as a dagger-thrust, their limbs twitching from their race to freedom, while, now in the distance, the Danes shouted again and again, like hounds on the scent of a frightened hare.

Chapter Two

Bolverk's Bargain

After a time all was quiet again, except for the swishing of rain on the roof of the forest which sent a steady whispering down the aisles of trees, but never reached the floor of age-dry pine-needles. This sound went on so long that at last Harald did not hear it. It became part of the silence.

And in this heavy quietness, with the smell of pine-cones in his nostrils, he remembered his dead brother Olaf again, and began to shake and shudder as though all his tears had dried up and this was his only way of weeping. Then his sorrow changed to wild fury and he dug his fingers deep among the pine-needles and clenched them time after time, as though he was clutching the throat of King Swein.

It was while he was doing this that a bird suddenly broke away from a near-by bush, and fluttered noisily up into the black tracery of forest-boughs, crying out in alarm.

Earl Rognvald, lying close beside Harald, whispered, 'That is a sign. The bird knows. They are coming. Lie still now or we are dead men.'

The Danes came openly into the wood, not bothering to be silent, but talking and laughing to one another as though they were going to a feasting. But nothing escaped them, and each man prodded with sword or spear into any bush or hummock of moss that could have sheltered a cat.

Harald glanced once at the Earl and saw beads of sweat covering the old man's face. Then he noticed that his own hands were streaming, as though he had dipped them into water.

After that he no longer had a chance to think of anything very much, because three men were making towards the bush under which he lay. He heard their shuffling feet pause, and he held his breath, hoping that his end would be a quick one. For a short moment, he almost jumped to his feet in the hope of striking one of them with his knife.

Then it was too late, because spear-points came slanting between the leaves and deep into the ground all about his head. Harald suddenly thought how hard and cruel they seemed, thudding beside him: very different from when he himself was guiding them at an enemy.

Under his breath, in a mortal fear, he whispered, 'Brother Olaf! Save me, Olaf!' He felt like a little child again, frightened in the dark, and not like a blooded warrior of fifteen who would one day be a king.

Suddenly the hard iron ran through his sleeve, pinning it for a space to the ground. Then another spear-point plunged between the fingers of his outspread hand. Harald stared at it in wonder, until it withdrew out of his sight. And while he waited for the next thrust, Earl Rognvald who lay close beside him gave a little start and clutched him tightly about the wrist.

And just as suddenly it was all over, and the Danes were moving away, laughing and joking and searching for another bush to poke into.

It seemed hours before the sound of their footsteps had

gone from hearing and the forest was its silent brooding self once more.

At last the Earl said hoarsely, 'We came well out of that, lad. One of those fools pushed his point into my leg, but I have had worse from a kicking cow in my time.'

Harald rolled over to answer him and then saw that the old man was lying still, as pale as death, his eyelids closed and blue. For a time he waited for the Earl to rouse again and speak, but when this did not happen, the lad went chill with fear and, pushing the low branches aside, he began to roll the body of his friend into the open, so that he could see the nature of his wound.

Earl Rognvald's leg-wrappings were dark and sodden, and now he began to groan as Harald moved him.

It was while the lad was cutting the breech-straps with his knife that he heard a sound behind him. Startled, on his knees, he turned to see a tall man wrapped in skins and carrying a rusty axe, gazing down at him, with a strange smile on his red-bearded face.

'Do not move,' the man said, 'or I will finish what the Danes began.'

Harald said in contempt, 'You are a Bonder dog, a jackal who follows the lion.'

The man shrugged his shoulders and answered, 'I saw that you were there all the while those stupid fellows were poking about in the bush. I could have told them where you were, Harald.'

The lad stared at him amazed. 'Are you a friend, then?' he said.

But the Bonder shook his matted head. 'No, not that,' he answered. 'I am what you said, a jackal. I take what the lion misses. If I told the lion what I knew, he would gobble it up, would he not? And I see that you and the old man carry good daggers and wear good mail-shirts. Why should Danes have those when Bonders need them?'

Harald began to judge the distance between the man and himself, but the Bonder nodded and said, 'My axe would fall on your neck before you could get to your feet. Be a wise fellow and give up your dagger. Perhaps it will buy your life and the life of the old Earl, if he still has a life to bargain for. Come, we will get him to my house, and perhaps, if Odin wills it, you may both escape my Danish friends.'

Harald said, 'A loyal friend you must be to any man!'

But the Bonder only laughed and said, 'In this life, as you will learn if you are given time, a man must do the best he can for himself. When it comes to feeding and clothing his family, or keeping his own neck out of the noose, a man cannot depend on Danes, or on anyone but himself. Come now, fling down your dagger and we will get the old man to shelter. He has a fever coming on him, I can see. We have no time to waste with such women's chatter.'

So they went on through the dark wood carrying Earl Rognvald, and always keeping an ear cocked for the sound of the questing Danes. Once, when they rested, the Bonder sang a song about Arsleif Summerbird, a strange chieftain of the Inner Lands, who once became King of the Bearfolk, after wrestling with the bear-champion and throwing him ten times before supper.

Harald was in no mood for such songs, and said so. But the Bonder shook his head and said, 'Princeling, you have much to learn still. Arsleif Summerbird is a greater man than any we have in the Northland. If you met him, you would feel your eyes popping out of their lids, and you would fall to your knees before him, thinking he was Odin.'

Harald, who was now very weary from fighting and sadness, answered, 'The only man I would bow before is my brother Olaf, and he is dead. There will never be such another, fellow, for God makes only one of that mould in a world's lifetime.'

The Bonder laughed shortly and said, 'Aye, Olaf was a good enough man, though overmuch concerned with praying to Christ for our liking, we up in the hill-lands. But wait till you have met with Arsleif Summerbird, then tell me what you think.'

At last they came to a hollow at the farthest edge of the pine-forest, and there tucked among bracken and hawthorn was a long log-house surrounded by a stockade with sharpened points. Sheep and cows and pigs were in the stockyard, and four shag-haired thralls to guard them. Blue smoke came up from the chimney-hole and grey pigeons sat on the roof-coping. The Bonder pointed and said, 'This is my place. This is where the old Earl can lie abed and get healed of his wound. My wife is a great hand at poultices, and if she can't cure him, then he is sick indeed.'

Harald glanced at the steading; it looked like a wooden fortress as much as anything. He said, 'Before we go in, how do I know that, tomorrow, you will not hand us over to the Danes, when you have stripped us of our mail-shirts?'

The Bonder blew through his lips and made a rude sound. 'If I had wanted your shirts, I could have taken them in the forest,' he said. 'Then I could have shown the Danes your bodies and got my reward for killing you, without any more trouble. Instead, I am bringing you to my house, and offering to put bread and meat into you until such time as you can make your own way abroad and save your skins. Does that sound like a traitor to you, Harald?'

The lad thought for a while, then said, 'Why should you go to this trouble, fellow, if you are not going to gain by it? Men do not use up their fodder and poultices unless there is gain to be had from it.'

The Bonder struck his axe-head into the ground and halted. 'Well, now,' he said lazily, 'you ask a fair question and I'll give you a fair answer. First, I love Danes no better than you do; but, like a ship, I have to go the way the wind blows. If the other Bonders go harnessed with Danes, then so must I, or have my house burned over my head and my kin put to the sword's edge. Second, your brother Olaf once stopped at my steading when he was out hunting, and gave my old woman a silver brooch from Miklagard in return for a cup of barley-beer – and of all the virtues, I cherish generosity in a man. But, best of all, and third – one day the dice may all fall otherwise, and who knows but what you might be a king yourself. Then, if you are anyway like your brother, you will say to yourself, "Ah, there was old Bolverk, who saved me and the Earl that day. He is a poor hard-working man and needs a new house and a score of milch-cows, and a dowry for his five daughters, and a fresh set of cooking-pots for his old wife. Ah, I'll look after old Bolverk, and mayhap I'll even see if he would like to be an Earl . . ." So that's what you will say, Harald.'

Harald stared hard at the Bonder and said slowly, 'Do you think so?'

Bolverk the Bonder pulled his axe out of the ground and smiled. 'No,' he answered, 'but it was worth putting to you. Come, then, and we will see what is cooking on the fire.'

And so Harald and Earl Rognvald came to the house of Bolverk the Bonder, and, as this man had promised, the Earl was healed of his deep leg-wound, and after a month or two had little more to show for it than a scar as long as his hand, and a limp that made him walk rather like a hobbled stallion. The worst Earl Rognvald had to tolerate after this was listening to the rough rhymes that Bolverk used to recite every evening. 'Do you know,' said Bolverk proudly one night after supper, 'about here, they call me Bolverk the Bard!'

'Then they must be fools – or deaf!' grunted the Earl.

The fight at Stiklestad happened in the July, and that was when King Olaf was killed. It was September before Earl Rognvald could walk without aid, and half-way through that month before he threw his blackthorn stick away.

The day he did this, he said to Harald, 'What now, lad? We must be doing. We cannot sit listening to Bolverk's nonsense much longer.'

Harald waited till the Bonder's wife had gone to the out-house, then he answered, 'It is our task to find Swein of Denmark, and to put a knife into his wicked heart. He has no right to rule in our land.'

But the Earl struck hard on the table-top and said, 'There, trust a rabbit to run back into the trap! You have no more sense than would fit snugly into a mouse's ear. Have we any weapons? Have we any war shirts? No! All we have is what covers us, and a pair of shoes on our feet.'

Harald flared up at the words about a mouse's ear, for he had grown up to think he was Olaf's heir both to land and wisdom. So he stood above the Earl and said, 'I shall remind you of this one day, Rognvald, and then you will see that there is no fool like an old fool.'

But the Earl was busy combing his beard with his finger-nails at that moment, and pretended not to hear; and when Harald's anger had died down, the Earl said, 'You have a kinsman, a cousin of some sort, who sits on the throne chair in Novgorod and calls himself Jaroslav. I have never seen Novgorod, though I have visited most places in the world. I have been to Dublin and London, and when I was a lad I sailed round Sicily. The best wine I tasted, though, was in

Jebel Tarik, where the women go about with their faces covered, and the men talk like monkeys. They have a tall rock there, and a nimble fellow could leap from its top into Africa – or so they tell me. But I've never yet set eyes on Novgorod, which is only in the next village, as you might say.'

Harald was still wondering whether the old Earl had lost his senses, when the Bonder came quietly through the door and said, 'I have been listening to what you were saying. I am a simple fellow and know more about milking cows and reaping barley than about these far-off places; but no man can ever say that Bolverk was not a man for a bargain.'

He came close and sat at the board with them, as though he was their equal. Then he said, 'Look you, in Novgorod there is great treasure. The Novgorod-men bring it back by the sledge-load from down south, where they get it from Bulgars, who get it from the weak-minded old Emperor at Miklagard. Now, we all know that Odin sets great store by a man who is out doing, and making his fortune, and not sitting back at home biting his finger-nails and helping his wife to wash the pots and pans. So, if I put you two in the way of getting the Novgorod treasure, then Odin would think of me as being a brisk fellow, too, would he not?'

Earl Rognvald sucked his lips together and gave a sly smile. 'You talk outside your knowing, fellow,' he said. 'First, we are not Odin-men any longer, as you must have heard. We are both baptized Christ-men. And second, how could the likes of you aid us in getting treasure, even if we wished?'

Bolverk scratched his shaggy head and said laughing, 'I was at Stiklestad like yourselves, and saw some of the fighting. And it did not occur to me that the Christ-men showed any more mercy than the Odin-men. So we can set that stuff aside for another buyer. And second, no man can gain treasure

unless he has a sword and a war-shirt, a horse and a saddle-bag full of food. Is that not so?'

The Earl said that it was so. Then Bolverk said, 'Very well, I will give you back your shirts and some weapons; and I will see that you have the other things, too. Which makes me a partner in the enterprise, does it not? And while you are away, I will make a poem about you!'

Harald was for refusing the offer straightway; but Earl Rognvald laid his withered hand on the boy's arm to silence him, and said, 'Yes, Bonder, it does. You shall have a third share of all we gain. Now get your wife to broach another keg of that voyage-ale she keeps hidden in the byre, and we will drink to the bargain. But no poems, please.'

When the laughing Bonder had gone away to see to this, the Earl said in a low voice, 'He is crafty, Harald, but we of noble blood are craftier. Once we are clear of this place, well-armed and horsed, we can suit ourselves whether we ever clap eyes on him again, treasure or no treasure.'

So Harald and the Earl and the Bonder drank merrily to the good luck of the Novgorod treasure-quest, and the next day the two set out over the hills, with their horses' noses reined towards Uppsala. It was a far journey they meant to make, but, as the Earl said to Harald, some of the war-men they had stood beside above Trondheim fiord had a still farther journey before them, up towards Heaven; which, as all men knew, lay off beyond Iceland, and was beset all the way by dragons, wolves with iron teeth, serpents with flame-casting eyes, and white-eyed women whose mere touch brought leprosy on a man.

Harald said, 'I have been thoughtless at times, Rognvald, and have often disputed your advice. Now, you must put that down to my youth and lack of teaching. From what you have told me, I now admit my stupidity. You have given much thought to this matter of religion, I can tell, and I will follow all your counsel from this time. We will go to Uppsala, and get aboard a stout ship there. Then we will take a look at Novgorod, and see if my kinsman, Jaroslav, leaves his treasure-chests unlocked at night.'

The Earl nodded, his face serious, and said, 'It is always a teacher's pleasure to hear that his wisdom has triumphed over the darkness that is in a youth's head. You will make a good king, yet, my boy.'

Harald laughed happily. 'But what about sharing the treasure with the Bonder, though?' he asked. 'We did make a bargain with him, you know.'

The Earl was by now feeling the stiffness coming back to his wound, and he said sharply, 'We will decide that matter when we are a few months older. As for me, I shall now look for a quiet place to lie down in, and shall sleep until some of the heat has gone out of the sun.'

Chapter Three

Sword from the Summerbird

The heat had well left the sun by the time the two travellers reached Uppsala, for by then it was late in October, and already the wind had icy teeth in it. But there they bartered the Bonder's horses for two places in a longship named *Thor's Larder* and began the long sea-way towards Finland.

It was not the smoothest of voyages. *Thor's Larder* belonged to two Swedish brothers, one short and red-haired, the other as stringy as a bean-pole and as white as snow, though he was younger than thirty. These two brothers were for ever at arguments and blows, for each claimed that the other had robbed him of his rightful inheritance when their father died. What was worse, they shared their quarrels with the others in the longship, forcing them to take sides in the most stupid of arguments.

One evening, the short red-haired man, whose name was Krok, came to Earl Rognvald and whispered behind his hand, 'If ever we see land, my friend, we shall be lucky men, for that brother of mine, Beanpole Spof, has no more notion of navigation than a cat has of playing the flute.'

Rognvald, who was never anxious to strike another man's blows for him without good payment, looked over the gunwales and said pleasantly, 'It is a fine sunset, tonight, ship-master. There are painters at Miklagard who would tear out their beards in rage, not to be able to put such a sight into a picture.'

Red-haired Krok came closer and said, 'You did not hear what I was saying, friend. I was saying that my brother . . .'

And Earl Rognvald said, 'Yes, oh, yes, ship-master. Down past Gardariké, a man would sooner paint a sunset glowing over the head of Saint Michael than he would eat his dinner.'

But Krok would not be put off. Taking the Earl's arm he stood on tiptoes and whispered hoarsely in his ear, 'With your aid, friend, I could pitch him overboard tonight, when the moon is down, and we could go on our way safely, for, as you must have noticed, I am the very prince of steersmen. When I am at the helm, we run against no shoals, and always seem to pick up the wind right at our backs.'

Earl Rognvald said, just as quietly, 'If you ever speak in that way to me again, I shall shorten you by a head's length – and a little fellow of your size could ill afford to lose any height. Be off with you!'

Later that evening, when the watch was changed, Bean-pole Spof came edging towards the Earl and said behind his hand, 'I must offer you my thanks, Earl. Do not think I do not know what went on. The brother of mine is always waiting to trip me up and so have this boat all for himself. Thank Odin he ran up against an honest man for once.'

Earl Rognvald said calmly, 'Your brother and I were discussing these painters at Miklagard. I was telling him what a fancy they have for painting sunsets, to put round their saint's heads for haloes. Now, as for me, though I am a Christian, as they call it, I would sooner put the paint on the planks of my longship to keep out the water. What do you say, ship-master?'

Beanpole Spof leaned down over the Earl and said urgently, 'You do not understand what I am telling you, friend. My fat little brother wants to kill me, don't you see? Now, if a good true man like you would only join me, together we could put him overboard off Estland, when everybody is asleep, and that would be the end of his wicked plotting.'

Earl Rognvald swung round suddenly, as though interested in the sea-birds, but so that his heavy sword-scabbard caught tall Spof across the shins, making him hop with the sharpness of the pain.

Then he said, as though to the birds which were circling the longship, 'If ever you come to me again with such ideas, I will nail you by the ears to the mast, to give us a new banner. Now be off with you!'

Harald heard all of this, and said with a smile, when Spof had scuttled away, 'Why do we not do what Harald Bluetooth would have done, and throw them both overboard? Then we could sail to Spain and see what the Moors have to give us.'

Earl Rognvald shook his head and answered, 'Harald Bluetooth was an old fool, lad. He was not fit to rule over a farm-midden, much less a kingdom. A ship got by trickery would never steer aright; and most likely it would founder before we had got it three lengths out into the waters. Besides, I have no taste for visiting the Moors again. My best friend lost both his thumbs and the end of his nose at Jebel Tarik, just for lifting a woman's face-veil to see if she was smiling or frowning at him.'

Harald said, 'And what was she doing?'

The Earl answered, 'Neither. She turned out to be the village simpleton, so no one could tell what she was doing. And that, you must agree, was a poor bargain for my friend, who never looked himself again.'

After that the Earl went under the after-deck and wrapped his cloak round him and was straightway off to sleep. He had this great gift, that whatever the weather, or the danger that threatened, he could always go to sleep without delay. Yet, on the other hand, if the danger came too close, Earl Rognvald was twice as fast as any other man at waking, though at this time he was a very old man, fifty if he was a day.

Thor's Larder was nearly a month coming towards Finland, but luckily much of the journey was beside the Estland coast, so that when the ale ran short, or the men felt sick, they could put ashore for the night. For Harald the trip seemed endless, but the old Earl comforted him and said, 'I have sailed this way when it has taken two months, lad. We are fortunate, for the west wind has been in our sail almost every day, pushing us onwards.'

Harald answered, 'I would rather walk five miles than sail one, west wind or not. If I never taste salt again, it will be too soon.'

Earl Rognvald put on a serious look and said, 'It is by way of being a tragedy that the King of Norway is no viking. The world has come to its last chapter when such a thing happens. Ah well, they are breeding a different race of men in the world today from what they were in my young ship-days.'

After that, Harald did his best to make up for what he had said. He even paid the oarsmen to hold out their blades stiff and still, while he ran the length of them, as the old vikings used to do, only two yards above the deep green water. But when he had done this, he got little praise from Rognvald, who turned away and said, 'So the King of Norway is a bigger fool even than old Bluetooth! What use would that foolery have been if you had fallen in? With your mail-shirt on, you would have slipped to the bottom faster than an iron coffer. Then who would have had to go in and fetch you out? Why, me, of course; for no one else among this crew of bleating sheep would risk his hide for a worthless lad.'

The Earl's anger lasted for three whole days, but then, when they were only a day from their port, something happened to put an end to it. That night, just when the land breeze was at its freshest and the moon had gone behind a cloud, Harald woke suddenly from his sleep to hear a sound like a bullock blurting. He turned towards the Earl and saw that the noise had wakened him, too.

So, bewildered, they both rose and went to the steerboard, where the sound had come from; and there they saw Beanpole Spof hanging over the gunwales with blood coming from him, and fat Krok still holding the axe that fetched forth the blood.

The Earl said, 'So it has come to this, has it? A brother has killed a brother. Well, now you have made it every man's affair, for this killing must be announced to the Thing when we reach the port. As the oldest man on board, I must ask you to place yourself in my charge.'

Then the Earl drew his sword and went forward to take the axe from Krok. But all at once the little fat man came out of his daze and, giving a great shout, he flung the red-stained weapon far into the sea, then began to cry out, 'Come quickly, my men! The old Earl has killed my dear brother and means to rob us of our ship!'

Before a man could count five fingers, the rowers had jumped up and were clustering so thickly round Rognvald and Harald that they could not have used their swords if they had wanted to.

It was Harald who pointed out to them all that Krok was lying, as could be seen by the fact that the Earl's sword-blade was unstained with blood. But Krok bawled out once more,

47

'See, the traitorous dogs! The old Earl wiped his sword on my poor brother's tunic after he had done the deed. Now hark at them, blaming me.'

The tallest of the oarsmen now came up and said gravely to Earl Rognvald, 'It ill becomes a nobleman of your fame to kill a poor fellow like Beanpole Spof. But we are rowers, not lawyers, and it will be for you to state your case at the Thing in Finland.'

So, by sheer weight of numbers, the oarsmen took away the swords of Harald and the Earl, and tied a rope loosely about their ankles, then flung them among the cargo as though they were sacks of barley-meal.

Later, under the after-deck, Harald said to the Earl, 'You called me a fool, old friend, but it might have been better after all if we had done what I first suggested, and had taken this ship down to Spain.'

But Earl Rognvald only smiled and said, 'If a pretty house-wife ran out of her kitchen every time a blackbird whistled, she'd never get any baking done.'

After that, Harald said no more, for he was more sure than ever that Rognvald was going mad because of his great age.

It was getting to be a bright morning now and the longship lay well into the shore. Harald could see a line of drift-wood huts, thatched with weed and sea-grass, with blue smoke coming from their chimney-holes, and children playing among the dogs outside the doors. Here and there were rough-coated men, tarring upturned boats, or splicing ropes. They looked up as the longship passed and either waved in casual greeting, or shouted out in hoarse voices that were more like those of hounds baying than men speaking.

Harald said in a quiet voice to the Earl, 'I see small mercy if we are handed over to fellows like this when we land.'

But Rognvald looked away and smiled up at the sky. 'They

are Finnfolk,' he said, 'and their law is different from ours. If you can quickly learn how to dance on your hands, or talk to the sea-mews, these Finns will side with you, rather than with the little fat man here.'

Harald said, 'But I cannot do those things, Rognvald. What then?'

The Earl leaned back on a bale of straw and said, 'Then we must find another way.'

As he spoke the men were all busy rowing, for the great sail had been furled so that the wind should not run the long-ship aground; and fat Krok was walking the length of the deck, occupied with the task of keeping the keel away from any drift-weed or hidden shoals.

He was standing, less than a yard from the Earl, and busy looking the other way, when suddenly Rognvald's tied feet swept out, knocking Krok sideways, off balance. As he fell to the deck, Harald took him by the throat and held him like a terrier with a rat. It all happened so fast that not even the foremost oarsmen saw what had taken place until it was too late. As the Earl grabbed Krok's knife and cut through their leg-bonds, the man yelled out for help; but even the most stupid rower knew that if he let go his oar, the other oars would knock against it and throw the whole ship out of time, perhaps even running her aground or tipping her over.

Krok knew this, too, and began to plead with the Earl. 'Have mercy, master,' he gasped. 'We did not mean to have you punished. It was a jest, I assure you!'

'And so is this,' shouted Rognvald, flinging the man with all his might against the mast-stepping. Then turning to Harald he said, 'Come, lad, over the side with you and let us see what the water is like this bright morning.'

Harald was down among the weed, spluttering, before he

had time to think. Then, with a great effort, he was striking up again to the sunlight, finding his iron shirt a great hindrance. As he broke surface, he saw the Earl only a few yards from him, swimming strongly, his face red and laughing and his white hair streaming behind him in the muddy waters.

Already the shouting from the longship was growing fainter, and Harald's heart was very light to think that he and the Earl had outwitted the Swedishmen. He began to hum a gay song as he swam, to beat time to his arm-strokes. Earl Rognvald turned back to him, still merry, and said, between gasps and spluttering, 'When you are King of Norway, lad, I will pay a skald to make a poem about this great swimming of yours. Not Bolverk, but a real poet! We must put our heads together when we land, and see what should go into such a poem. You know what these bards are for getting the wrong end of the stick. We must put them right.'

Harald was still listening to the Earl's breathless words when a shrill whirring sounded in the air over his head from the direction of the longship. Then suddenly Rognvald almost leapt right out of the water, like a salmon breasting a hillside stream.

'What is it friend?' called the boy, his mouth half-full of salty water. Now Earl Rognvald's strokes were slower and slower, and soon he was swimming with his face below the sea. Harald gained on him, and then saw that the water about the Earl was reddening as though a dye had been poured into it. And as he noticed this strange happening, his ears caught the vicious sound of other arrows *chucking* into the shoal-water all about him, throwing up sharp spurts of white before they clove down out of sight.

But Harald paid no heed to these arrows now. Soon he was beside the Earl, and then his feet touched the bottom and he found he could stand. But Earl Rognvald did not stand; he lay face-downwards, his arms spread wide, and his white hair floating above him.

A shag-haired man came running, knee-deep in water, towards them, a fish-spear in his right hand, a thin black dog close behind him yelping with excitement.

Harald called to him, 'Give me a hand, fellow, to drag the Earl to the shore.'

The man reached down and put his arms about Rognvald, then shook his head and said, 'He will swim no more. The man who loosed that arrow must know good prayers to offer. I wish I could aim as well.'

Now other men came, clustering round, and all helping to lift the Earl's body up and get it on to the muddy shore. Harald could only gaze at the pale face that had been ruddy and laughing but a few moments before. And to himself he kept on saying, 'But this is not just. We were talking about a poem, and then he said no more. It is not just.'

An old man whose head was wrapped with furs and who leaned heavily on a blackthorn stick, came to the front of the crowd and said in a thick voice, 'Stop babbling, boy, and answer a few questions. I am the headman here and I must be told all that happens.'

Harald said hotly, 'Then I tell you that Earl Rognvald, the companion of kings, has just been murdered by Krok the Swede. It is your duty not to stand doddering there on a stick, but to catch that longship when it pulls in to shore, and to punish the murderers of my friend.'

The old man turned away from Harald and said, 'The lad's a fool. If we as much as lay a finger on a Swedish longship, next season we shall find our houses burned about our heads, and our children driven off into slavery. Strip the Earl of his shirt and make a hole for him on the shore. As for the lad, we'll offer him for sale to the next party of fur-traders to come along the coast. He looks strong enough and he'd make a good sledge-puller for some trader short of dogs.'

Though Harald fought and kicked out with all his force, the shore-folk were too many for him, and they carried him, weeping with fury, up towards the row of smoke-blackened huts. In the distance, he saw *Thor's Larder* pulling away, well offshore now, towards a point where the thick pinewoods came down almost to the sea.

Shaking his fist in anger, he called out, 'Ill luck go with you, Krok! I'll pay you back for this day's work if I have to spend my lifetime doing it!'

As he was saying this, a tall dark-faced man came to the door of a hut over which a bush hung, indicating that here was an inn for travellers. His hair fell down on to his breast and his hands were long and fine, their fingers bright with gold and silver rings. His sharp black eyes, his hooked nose, and his oiled and curly beard, made him look like a hawk, or an eagle; but his clothing was of so many and such fine colours, reds and yellows and greens, that there was no hawk and no eagle ever so gaily-garbed.

This man stared at Harald a moment, then said, 'Spirit in hound, horse, and lad is good to see; but a weeping boy is neither use to God nor man.'

Harald stopped shouting and turned towards the man. He was the tallest man the lad had ever seen, taller even than King Olaf.

'What is your name, fellow?' he asked, putting on his sternest face, and wishing the tears did not still run down his cheeks.

The tall man walked over to him and, with one of his bright red sleeves, wiped Harald's face dry. He did it so calmly and so gently that not even the wildest baresark could have taken offence at the gesture.

Then he bent his head and looked down at Harald and said softly, 'My name is Arsleif, and the folk inland call me Summerbird, because, as you see, I go gaily garbed.'

Harald looked him up and down, remembering what Bolverk had said of Arsleif Summerbird. Then he answered, 'You and I are kings, or as good as kings. This dead man was my friend, Earl Rognvald, right-hand of Olaf the King. So, do you wonder that I weep?'

Arsleif Summerbird pinched his thin lips together and then answered, 'To lose your brother and your best friend, as you have done, is a heavy burden for any man to bear; but letting salt water run out from between the eyelids lightens no load.'

For a moment, Harald began to hate this tall man, but then Arsleif Summerbird smiled and said, 'It is the task of every man to learn how to bear his grief without weeping. I was twenty before I learned this, and by that time I had lost so many kinsmen and friends that there was no more salt water left in my head. So, you will learn it, as I did. And you will learn that I too have a score to settle with fat Krok, who robbed me of a fur-cargo less than a year ago, taking my best skins and paying me with wormy meal and sour ale. You will come with me, and one day we may meet this Swedishman again, and have a short talk on business matters with him.'

Harald said, 'You will make me a thrall to pull your sledges? Is this what you mean?'

Arsleif Summerbird smiled and said, 'I shall give the headman here a few marks for your ransom, as one king to another; and I shall take you with me, fur-trapping, towards Novgorod, where I hope to sell in the markets at the depth of winter, which is the time when my furs fetch the best prices.'

Overcome by his feelings, Harald clasped the tall man's

hand and began to shake it as though he was the oldest friend he had.

Arsleif Summerbird said, 'Enough is enough, my young friend. One would think that Novgorod was where you most wanted to be. But there are other places, too, and we will visit them all, if we are spared.'

That evening, in the inn, Harald and Arsleif Summerbird ate and drank with the fur-traders, when they had seen that Earl Rognvald's body had been decently buried, with a stone above it to mark where it lay.

And before the night was out, Arsleif Summerbird unwrapped a bright sword from a bundle of sheepskins and gave it to Harald.

'This sword,' he said, 'comes from Toledo in the land of the Moslems. It is so sharp that it will run through the best mail-shirt any smith has ever forged. And it is of iron so tough that you could strike against a rock all day with it, and never spoil its edge. I was keeping it for my own son, when he grew to warrior-hood, but while I have been here by the shore, selling my furs, word has come to me that my son has been taken from me by a plague. It is not my place to mourn, for in my village every house has lost its children. I am fortunate to find another son so soon. So I give you my son's sword, and welcome. Its name is *Whitefang*, and that name must stay with it, or it loses its edge. Are you content?'

Harald took the sword, *Whitefang*, and was so full of feeling that he almost wept over it; but Arsleif Summerbird pushed the bright blade away, so that tears should not fall on it. 'There, lad,' he said, 'a little toy like that is no cause for grief. See that no tears ever blunt its blade. That is the secret the old swordsmith told me, in Moslemland, when I got this sword. It can tolerate any amount of blood and wine, but not a single tear.'

When Harald went into the byre, to sleep among the straw, he wondered whether Arsleif Summerbird had made up this story to cure his sadness, but before he could make up his mind, he was fast asleep; and when the fur-traders woke him the next morning, so that they could make an early start, the thought had gone out of his mind, leaving only a great gratitude that things should have fallen out so well. It was a bright crisp morning, with an early frost already on the thatched roofs of the huts. It was such a day as all heroes pray for, when they set out on their great adventures. All the same, he felt his sadness again for a little while, when they passed the old Earl's grave-mound by the shore.

Chapter Four

Fur-train to Novgorod

The east road to Novgorod was no way for a weakling to take. Up along the rushing river, where the rocks gave the sledges great trouble, both horses and oxen could founder; and there were marshes which gave no sign of their presence, except that the grass above them was slightly greener than anywhere else. Even some of the most experienced fur-traders found trouble there. It was a land almost always covered in a grey mist, that only thinned out at midday when the sun came down at its hottest. Then the light lasted for no more than an hour, and Arsleif Summerbird always gave orders that the tents should be staked and the day's journey ended.

For Harald it was magic-land. Once, among the sighing pinewoods that clustered close beside the rushing river, he saw great vague shapes of horned creatures; and when he asked what they were, Arsleif Summerbird told him that they were the first of the cattle, the Great Ox that had been there since the beginning of the world. They were immense beasts, and seemed to brush the highest boughs of the pinewoods with their long horns. Harald dreamed of them for nights afterwards.

Then the snow began to come, to bring him other bad dreams and night-fears. At first, it fell lightly, like swan's down, just here and there, causing no distress to man or beast. Then gradually it came harder and harder until, at last, as the long line of fur-traders made its way across the plain, it was like the thickest sort of arrow-hail, sharp and stinging, making the world all white, hurtful to the eyes and face. Even the hardiest of the dogs which always went with the fur-traders shrank from this hard snow-shower, and scuttled with their tails between their legs to the end of the winding column.

Arsleif Summerbird took off his coloured clothes and put on a hood and shirt and breeches of deerskin. Only his black eyes could be seen when he drew down the peak of his head-gear.

One day Harald said to him, 'Arsleif Summerbird, where do you come from? You are like no man I have ever seen before.'

Arsleif Summerbird whistled like a thrush for a while in the driving snow, then turned to the lad and said, 'I have had that question asked many times before. And often I have killed the man who asked it.'

Harald was tucked up warm in his own new deerskin shirt

and hood; he was switching at his legs with a little twig, and he was not afraid of anyone. He said, 'Very well, then I ask you this time, and I dare you to kill me!'

Arsleif Summerbird said, 'You know what you are doing. The others asked out of vulgar gossip's sake; but you are my adopted son and you know I cannot withhold anything from you.'

Harald said, 'Since my brother Olaf died, and my hand-friend Rognvald went under the water, you are the only one I love. So I do not see why I should not ask you anything, or tell you anything. Very well, where do you come from, Arsleif-father Summerbird?'

The leader of the fur-traders scratched at his arm as though the gnats were at it, which was not possible in that cold place and at that cold time. Then he said, rather laughing in his throat, lightly, as though it was a thing to be pleasant about, 'I am from Tarifa, where a man can jump from the high rock into Africa. I am a Moor, as they say up here. Does that settle the question?'

Harald nodded then marched on a while before he said, 'So you pray to Allah?'

Arsleif Summerbird said, 'Yes, I go on to my knees three times a day, in general; five times a day, when there is leisure to do so. But I have been up and down the world, son, and I have seen many men praying to their different gods in different ways; so, although I know that the Odin-men and the Christ-men are misled, I do not deny them those rights which I claim myself. Some of the fellows in this camp of fur-traders are Finns who pray to some witch or other. And there are Germans who carry a bone from a horse's head in their pouches, to worship. I care not, if the man works well and gets his catch of fox-skins and otter-pelts. God is god; there is only one god, and his name is Allah. The horse's head and the witch and the Christ, they are all a simple man's way of trying to reach out to Allah.'

Harald said, 'I am not so sure of that, Arsleif Summerbird. But I will give it my consideration when I have the time.'

Arsleif nodded gravely, then said, 'I was only seventeen when the pirates carried me off to Aachen, to sell me to the Franks. I was hunting by the shore with my sister on a white Arab stallion, no doubt showing off, as was my habit in those days. We were, you understand, the children of the Caliph. So we thought the world was an easy place to live in. We thought that life lasted for ever, and that it was always summer. Then suddenly the pirates came over the cliff-top and pulled me off my horse. My sister galloped back to the fort to rouse our people, but it was too late. The pirates slung me into their longship together with sheep and goats and had me away as neatly as a boy traps a rabbit. Then, at Aachen, an old German bought me as his kitchen-boy. Finding me a sharp young fellow, he had me taught Latin and such nonsense, and when I was twenty, sent me to escort his daughter on a pilgrimage to a shrine near Antioch. That place would have suited me splendidly, but I had other plans. I spoke to the Captain of the Guard there, telling him I had a strong German girl for sale. And so I gained enough ready money to set myself up in the fur-trade.'

Harald was shocked. 'You sold your master's daughter?'

Arsleif Summerbird said, '*Ojalá*, but you sounded just like the priest who taught me Latin, then! A very red-nosed pious man, who thought the fate of the world depended on the right use of the accusative! Yes, son, I sold the German girl; which was tit for tat, in a way, for the pirates selling me, and the German buying me. I have led a good life since then, and have bought and sold no one else. You recall, I did not even buy you. I just paid your freedom-money. So I consider that

I stand fairly well in the sight of whatever god rules in whatever land I wander in.'

Harald said no more for a while. He had enough to be thinking about. Then the snow came really hard, carried on a wind strong enough to blow a stone house down. The fur-traders were three weeks laid up among the rocks by the river's side, snuggling in the crevices like weasels, coughing and spluttering with all manner of chest troubles. In the third week two of them died from lack of food; the others cursed the winter, coming so silently, like a spy at a feast, with a knife in its hand.

Arsleif Summerbird did not like them to curse so much, and would often call them together and lecture them on correct behaviour. After which they would be better for a while, and would suffer their hunger more graciously. Then the rushing river ran slower, and at last stopped because it was all ice. So it became difficult to get water to drink, and once more the men grew impatient.

Arsleif Summerbird told them to melt the ice over their fires; and though it was not the same as fresh water, it served well enough.

One dark night, when the fur-train was well on the way to Novgorod, and there were now no trees at all, and no rocks either, but only wide grey expanses of plainland, Arsleif Summerbird said to Harald, 'My son, this last hour I have been troubled with such a strange feeling that I think my fate is coming to fetch me. Do not be troubled, but if this should happen, I want you to succeed me as leader of this fur-train; and I want you to take the five wooden chests which are in the last sledge, and keep them for your inheritance. They are full of silver and gold, and goblets and necklaces, and such priests' and women's things. Some of them have come from Miklagard, some from Jerusalem, and some from Andalusia. It is all treasure rightly got, so you need have no fear about taking it. I think it timely to say this to you, because of the strange feeling I have.'

Harald was now greatly alarmed and said, 'What is this strange feeling, Summerbird? Is it in the arms or legs or body? Is it a chill?'

Arsleif lifted the hood of his deerskin coat and smiled. 'It is nowhere,' he answered. 'It is only that when I walk out beyond the sledges, I feel that there are eyes staring at me from behind. So the back of my head twitches and the skin on my back crawls. That is all.'

Harald said, 'All men must feel like that, in this howling plain with wolves creeping about in the dusk. Look, let us go outside together, and leave this bright fire in the cave; and we will tell one another the moment we feel it. Then we may discover what it is that troubles you.'

So they did this, and walked away from the cave, and out of reach of the fires. And at a spot where the last sledge was stationed, where there were no men at all to be seen, Arsleif Summerbird said, 'Now, I feel it here!'

Harald, who walked beside him, nodded and said, 'So do I. It is as though men were standing behind me, watching every step I took and wondering whether to shoot their arrows at me now, or a little later.'

Arsleif began to laugh and said, 'Well, if we both feel like that, let us be brave and turn round, to frighten these ghosts away, and so prove to ourselves that we are men.'

So they both turned round; and in the dusk before them they saw a long line of horsemen, sitting silently in their high sheepskin saddles, each one holding a drawn bow, and each one staring from out of their fur-hoods like Northland spirits.

Arsleif Summerbird laughed and said, 'This gives me much

relief son. When I came to the cave, I was certain that I was going to die. Now I only think I might do!'

As he spoke, one of the horsemen grunted an order to his fellows, and the long line plunged forwards, reaching out their arms to sweep Harald and Arsleif Summerbird into the saddles before them.

Chapter Five

Jaroslav's Yuletide Feasting

For a while, all was a whirl of hooves and scattering snow. The world turned upside-down for Harald; there was dark sky with a moon in it at his feet, and bushes and boulders over his head.

Then, as the shaggy ponies galloped on and on, and he found a firmer seat in the slippery saddle, sense returned to the world, and he saw more clearly what was happening.

And what he saw now was as amazing as what he had seen before.

Arsleif Summerbird was sitting, two-up with a squat fur-clad rider, hunched like a dwarf on his horse's back, and was slapping the old man's shoulders and laughing as though he had found an old friend.

Harald called out above the thrumming hooves, 'What is going on, Arsleif-father?'

His friend pulled back the deerskin hood and yelled, 'These blind fools thought I was some rich trader they could rob – and find that instead I am only their old visitor, the Summerbird, who has sold in their Novgorod markets for half a lifetime!'

Harald, still bewildered, cried, 'Then will they set us down and let us mind our own business?'

Arsleif answered, 'Not if I can arrange it! Riding with them, we shall reach the city in half the time. Our trappers can follow on at their own snail-speed, and good fortune to them!'

And so it was that Harald and Arsleif Summerbird came to Novgorod, in the bitter winter weather, with nothing more in their hands than they could carry, but with hearts as light as spring blackbirds. And at Novgorod, they found that King Jaroslav was about to hold his Yuletide feast, and that his great rambling wooden palace was blazing with white fat-candles, enough to light any common house for three years.

King Jaroslav, Grand Duke of Novgorod, Prince of Kiev, King of the Plains and cousin to Sigurdson, sat on his gilded pine-wood throne to receive Harald and Arsleif Summerbird; and he wore gold and jewels enough on him to weigh down any ordinary man. But Jaroslav was built in Thor's own mould; his forearms were as thick as most men's thighs; his neck was nearly as round as a girl's waist; his hands were so big that he must have his drinking-cup made of iron, for any lesser metal crumbled when he gave the toast. And as though these were not enough great qualities for any king to possess, it was said that his black beard grew so strongly that, during any silence in the feast-hall – which did not happen often – an alert man might truly hear his whiskers pushing outwards, as thick as the bristles on a broom. One skald made a song which said that when King Jaroslav was angry – which was three times a day, except in the cold winter-weather which slowed all things down – his eyes stood out from their lids as big as apples, and the veins in his neck pushed up as stoutly as the hempen ropes of a longship's rigging.

King Jaroslav smiled down as Harald kneeled before him

and said, 'Greetings, young cousin. Get up off that stone floor or we shall have you in bed with an ague. Come and sit beside me on this chair; after all, you will soon be a king, and there is room enough for two here, since your good old aunt died.'

So Harald sat beside the King and told him all about the battle at Stiklestad, where holy King Olaf died, while Arsleif Summerbird sat on a lower step of the dais and drank cup after cup of warm spiced berry-wine.

And when Harald had finished his tale, King Jaroslav said, 'That Swein could do with a sword in him. It would make a better man of him. I am too occupied at the moment with my own wicked peasant-farmers, who hate paying their rightful dues and taxes, otherwise I would relish the idea of sailing to Denmark and eating him up.'

Then, seeing that this matter was a painful one for Harald, King Jaroslav changed the topic and clapped his hands for servants to bring the Princess Elizabeth to meet her cousin from Norway.

Elizabeth was only thirteen, but she was as tall as most of the women at the court. Her face was very pale, and her hair was long and thick, light yellow in colour, and done into six braided plaits round her head. Her eyes were a faded blue, almost grey, though her eyebrows were quite dark. This gave her an expression as though she was either frowning or mocking, most of the time. Her nose was thin and pointed, and her mouth was most often set in a downward curve, as though she was smiling at some secret thought which amused her. All told, she was like no girl Harald had ever seen before; nor did she walk meekly, like the girls in Norway, waiting to be spoken to first, before she dared open her own mouth.

Instead, as soon as she set foot within the audience chamber, she pointed her long forefinger at Arsleif and said,

'Who gave this monkey the right to sit at the King's feet?'

Then she turned her light eyes on to Harald and pointed at him saying, 'And who told you to sit on the King's chair, jackanapes?'

King Jaroslav coughed behind his great hand and said mildly, like a wolf that has swallowed butter to make his voice sweet, 'Ah, come, my love, come my sweeting, and give your cousin from Norway a big kiss.'

Princess Elizabeth paused in her tracks, looked searchingly at Harald, then gave a loud sniff and said, 'I should think not! Why, I would sooner kiss our cat than that whey-faced boy! Look at him, with his great red wrists all dangling out of his sleeves and his great big feet all covered with mud. And look at his great big head, and his great big nose, and his thick hair all shaggy. It wants the woodcutters' chopper on it, that hair of his! Who does he think he is, to come into a King's house with bracken for hair? And I bet it's as full of fleas as our dog's back!'

King Jaroslav was so taken aback that he gave a great thump on his chair-arm and broke a lion's head off the carving, which angered him still more. Arsleif Summerbird was so amused both at the girl's sauciness and the King's broken lion that he drank his berry-wine down the wrong way and was beside himself with spluttering. As for Harald, he leapt up from the throne chair and almost ran at the girl, saying, 'Call yourself a princess! Why, I have seen better manners in the pig-market at Oslo on a Friday morning.'

By now, King Jaroslav had regained his composure and said, 'Daughter, this young prince has been in a great battle. He has also outwitted the Swedish pirates; and what is more, he has come on foot through the bad deep snow all the way down to Novgorod. There are many heroes who have not done half as much.'

68

Princess Elizabeth came closer to Harald and said, 'And there are many who have done much more. As for walking across to Novgorod through the snow, he must be stupid. And come to think of it, he *looks* stupid, standing here and shaking his fists at me. For he knows he daren't lay a finger on me.'

King Jaroslav suddenly lost his good humour again, and he called out, 'Go on, Harald, you have my permission to give her a slap for her bad manners. She has been allowed too much freedom since her mother died. I am glad that we now have a young man of equal rank with her to teach her how a princess should behave. Go on, Harald, I command you to give her a smacking. I am never quick enough to catch her.'

Now Harald was more upset than before. It is one thing to be furious on the spur of the moment, but quite another to be angry because a King orders it. Suddenly Princess Elizabeth burst out laughing and said, 'Look the silly goose does not know which way to turn, between you and me! Very well, I will settle this quarrel, which amounts to nothing after all, and will let him kiss me in cousinly greeting.'

She stepped forward a pace, and held her face sideways. Harald would rather have been in the battle beside old Rognvald, or hiding under the bush when the Danes came foraging with their spears. But Arsleif Summerbird called out, 'Come, Northman, show us how a viking treats these forward women!'

So Harald had to go forward and kiss the Princess in greeting, though he went as red as fire when Elizabeth very carefully wiped the kiss off, and then ran to her father and began to tug at his iron beard in play.

King Jaroslav put up with this as long as he could, then he sent the girl away; and when she was out of sight, he said to Harald, 'It was your brother Olaf's wish that you should one day marry my daughter. Well, now you have seen her, and you know what lies in store for you. What have you to say?'

Harald looked down at his feet, not wishing to offend this great King, and said at last, 'It is a matter on which I have had little time to think, Cousin-King. All my time has been taken up learning sword-play and axe-play and the management of horses.'

King Jaroslav said pleasantly, 'That is as it should be. And doubtless you have learned, from taming horses, something that will be of use to you when it comes to taming this girl. So your time has not been wasted. Now go with Arsleif to our guest-house and make ready for the feast. There will be time enough after that is over for us to talk about betrothals and marriages. Go with a light heart, cousin.'

If Harald's heart was not light when these words were spoken, it was so when he entered Jaroslav's feast-hall, for he had not seen so many merry folk gathered together at Yuletide in the whole of his life. They sat along two long tables, the length of the spruce-lined hall; men of all nations – big raw-boned chieftains from the Baltic coast, red-haired lords from outside Kiev, and even small, dark, slant-eyed men whose beards were smaller than a goat's and who would not take off their fur caps even in the King's presence. Where these last men came from, Harald could not find out, but one of them brought a small bear in with him, shackled by a silver chain, and laughed in a high voice when this animal nibbled at the legs of the feasters sitting opposite him: so, at least, Harald thought, they must be witty men, wherever their homes were.

King Jaroslav sat in a great chair, under the shields on the gable wall, in the middle of a table set cross-wise. Though it was not the custom for palace-women to attend such feasts, for fear they caused trouble, Elizabeth sat at his left hand, her hair now tucked up and looking, in her deerskin jacket, very much like a boy. Harald was at the King's right hand, with Arsleif Summerbird beside him, as the special guests of Novgorod that Yuletide.

Harald whispered to Arsleif, 'It would suit me better if that girl had stayed in her bower.' But Arsleif only laughed and said, 'Once the Yuletide ale has passed this way a time or two, such thoughts will fly from your mind like clouds before the wind.'

No man could ever accuse King Jaroslav of meanness when it came to providing feast-fare. When all were seated, he banged on the table with the bone haft of his meat-knife to bring order, then he stood and called out in a loud voice, 'Here ye, friends, hear ye! It is our custom that no edged tools shall be used in this hall, save for the purpose of cutting up meat. Moreover, so that you shall keep this Yuletide holy and free from all strife, it is my command that any wound caused among you by meat-knife, ale-cup, meat-bone, or fist shall be regarded as outright murder and shall be punished by hanging!'

There was some muttering and mumbling at these words, because not a few of the men there had come in the pious hope of meeting neighbours who had stolen their cattle or burned their byres out of spite. But the great troll-king glared down the tables with his eyes wide open like apples, and soon the whispering was still again. Then King Jaroslav raised his iron cup, from which the ale already flowed as he moved it, and called for three toasts: to the honour of Christ, to the good fortune of Jaroslav, and to the return of the sun. Harald's sharp eyes saw that though all men drank to Christ, not a few of them made the sign of the hammer, with clenched fist over their cups, before drinking. These were men from outlying parts, who still held to Thor. He noticed also that

71

though Arsleif Summerbird raised his horn with all the others, his lips were not wet when the cup came away; but then the many servants began to bustle about the hall and Harald had no chance to mention this to his friend.

Three tall lords, with high-domed heads and no hair upon their faces, save for long moustaches, men whose skin was as pink as coral, but whose arms were like great hams, began to hammer the tables with their fists and shout out, 'Where is the food we were promised, Jaroslav? Have we come all this way from the Baltic to dine on bones?'

Jaroslav nodded to them mildly, then hissed at the thralls to run round to that table immediately with the Yuletide fare. Turning to Harald, he whispered, 'They are three chieftains from the Baltic shore, three brothers, who will bow the knee to no one, but who travel up and down the world from one feasting to another, till they are as fat as butter. It grieves my heart to see so much good food go down their throats, I tell you, nephew.'

Harald said, 'Why don't you send them packing, then?'

King Jaroslav's eyes widened in astonishment at these words. 'Oh no! Oh no!' he said, his voice small with shock. 'If I turned them out, the Brothers Blutkind, I could look to lose my throne and perhaps my head before next corn-springing! They boast that though they are not kings, they make and unmake kings. They say that if they but climb the nearest tree, where they are, and blow upon their bone whistles, five hundred men come running out of the grass to ask what needs doing. No, lad, it is better to feed them and put up with their taunts.'

By now, Harald was scarcely listening, for the food-thralls had come to his end of the table and were serving out the Yuletide fare. Some carried wooden troughs of sausage, of which each man received an arm's length, or more if he needed it; others hauled steaming pots, full of thick broth in which floated great hunks of meat. On clay plates down the board were set bread-cakes and fried turnips; and near the end of each table stood a butt of ale. But best of all were the huge trenchers of acorn-fed hog-meat, for Jaroslav had had fifty-six pigs slaughtered for this feasting, and that was eight pigs better than Harald Bluetooth had ever offered in his fortress at Jellinge.

This pork was so fat that it slid down the throat, almost before a man had the chance to bite at it; and the crackling was so crisp that one of the Baltic chiefs suddenly jumped up and shouted, 'Oh, crackling my dear, my beloved! Where else is there a sweetheart as comely as you? Whose hair is as bright as your crispy-brown? Whose cheeks are so shiny with fat? Oh, dear crackling!'

His brothers began to slap him on the back, saying, 'Oh, dear crackling!' in mockery. Then they all began to laugh, and twisting their arms about each others', drank from one another's cups and horns. At last they fell backwards off their benches and lay laughing in the straw.

Harald saw that some of the yellow-faced chiefs wasted none of their pork, but even rubbed their hands on their black hair, when the meat was done. He also saw that Arsleif Summerbird most carefully avoided touching it, but nudged it gently to the side of his wooden plate with the back of his knife, so that none of the fat should come near his lips in eating.

Then another thing called his attention away; a dwarf with no head or arms suddenly jumped out of the curtains on to the middle table, and began to dance on one spot, shooting out his legs before him so fast that it seemed as though he was sitting on air, just a foot above the board. Everyone was amazed and silent. Even the three Baltic chieftains crawled up to peer at this marvel with their big blue eyes, their pale hair hanging in great plaits on to the table.

At the far end of the hall, near the fire, a girl with raven hair, stuck full with cock's feathers, dyed blue and red and white, was thrumming on a little lute, making the strings hum and howl and twitch, as her long dark fingers shivered over them like summer lightning. Some of the men forgot the dwarf and began to throw gifts to this girl, calling her the Queen of lute-players, and the Princess of Melody. Some said she was Freya, but others argued that Freya's hair was corn-coloured, and that this girl was Marienna of the Sumerians come back to earth again. One of the Baltic chieftains staggered down the hall saying that he would ask for her hand in marriage, and, if need be, would kill any ten men who tried to stop him. But he did not need to go to such trouble, for, half-way down the hall, he suddenly fell down and began to snore, his long plaits coming near to getting burned off in the hearth-fire that blazed with holly-logs and pine.

Arsleif Summerbird said, 'Jaroslav's ale is the best in the North, they say. Yet it ill becomes a man of property to guzzle it until he has not more wit than a scarecrow.'

One of the other Baltic brothers heard Arsleif's last words, and came across the room to him, clutching his meat-knife in his great ham-like hand.

'Would you say that my brother is a mawkin for frightening crows, outlander?' he asked, his mouth shiny with fat.

Arsleif Summerbird cut himself a piece of fried turnip and held it by his lips, as though thinking. 'No,' he answered, 'I would not say that.'

The Baltic chieftain began to laugh, swaying on his feet, and holding his head back so that his thick plaits hung down behind him like ship's ropes.

'Then what would you say of my brother?' he asked.

Arsleif Summerbird frowned a little, then he smiled and answered.

'I would say that if he had twice the wit he has shown to-night, then he might be a mawkin's apprentice and, in time, come to frighten a very small sparrow.'

The Baltic chieftain stared at Arsleif Summerbird, his pale blue eyes as empty as winter rock-pools, his pink face straining to shape itself into an expression of understanding. At last he said thickly, 'If it were not for the King's Yuletide law, I would come round this table and brain you with a pork bone.'

Arsleif Summerbird laughed up at him and said, 'Then you would be doing both me and yourself a great wrong, lord. For you would be killing an honest man, and causing a brave one to hang.'

For a while the pale-eyed man gazed at Arsleif, as though unable to see him clearly. Then his broad face wreathed with smiles and he spluttered, 'You call me a brave man! Aye, that I am – a very brave man. And that makes you a very honest man, my friend. For he who tells the truth is a very honest man, and I will kill any man who denies me that.'

Suddenly he glared at Harald and said, 'Do you deny me that?'

Harald solemnly shook his head and said, 'I do not deny you that. Of course you are a brave man, to eat as much as you have done, and to drink the King's ale as though it were water. Only a very brave man would so risk stifling and drowning at one time!'

The Baltic chieftain stopped laughing and, leaning with both hands on the table, stared down at Arsleif and Harald, his eyes now filling with tears.

'To have lived so long,' he said, shaking his head with happiness, 'to have heard such talk at Yuletide from men I do not even know! This is truly the season of brotherly love, as the priests said. You two are my friends, for life. Each Yuletide we shall sit at the board and you shall tell me of my bravery. Now I will join you at your side of the table, and will sit between you.'

But as he staggered forward, one of the kitchen-dogs ran between his legs, chasing a cat, and tumbled him over. Four thralls ran forward and dragged him down the hall to where his brother lay, still snoring.

Arsleif whispered, 'With friends like him, a man needs no enemies!'

But Harald's eyes were on the dwarf again, who had suddenly cast off the sheepskin bag that had covered his head and his arms, and had grown to be as tall a man as any there, laughing and singing as the lute still strummed, as busy as a bower-bird.

Elizabeth bent towards Harald and said, 'Get up on the table, cousin, and see if you could do as well.'

Harald's face flushed again at her teasing, but he kept his patience and only answered, 'There are trades for every man, and dancing is not my trade.'

Elizabeth smiled thinly and replied, 'What is your trade, then, cousin?'

Harald, a little warm in the head from the feasting, said airily, 'Oh, a bit of this and a bit of that. A tussle with a bear or a tumble with an ox!'

'Then here's your chance cousin,' suddenly said Elizabeth, her eyes half-shut with mockery.

And as she spoke, two young men leaped over the far table from out of the dimness and called, 'We are Icelanders. Our names are Wulf Ospakson and Haldor Snorreson, and we challenge any man between fifteen and fifty to try three throws against us.'

'Now is your chance, as I said,' whispered Elizabeth, pointing her long finger at Harald.

Arsleif Summerbird laid his hand on Harald's arm and said gently, 'I have seen young fighting-cocks like this before. Iceland breeds them by the score, and they seldom come away from home but to gain fame among these simple folk with their rough play. Do not let this girl egg you on to get a broken arm or a twisted neck, my son. Suffer her taunts, and go whole to bed tonight.'

But Harald was too far gone in anger against Elizabeth now to listen to the Summerbird's wise counsel, and before he knew what he was doing, he too had leaped the board, and, tugging his feasting-tunic off, cried out, 'I'll take on either of you, for three throws or six.'

Now all was silent in the hall, for it was at such times that a man might look to see something he might tell his grandchildren of. Even Elizabeth was still, her eyes wide, her hands placed over her mouth, as though she had got more than she bargained for, and was not sure whether she cared for the bargain after all.

One of the Icelanders, a thick-set, red-haired youth, called, 'I am Wulf Ospakson, and I will take you first, Norway.'

Then, from behind Harald a great voice sounded, 'I am not yet fifty, so I will take your mate, Icelander!'

And there was Arsleif Summerbird, stripped to the waist and striding beside Harald, grinning like a baresark, his hawk's nose jutting out before him as though he was going to pick the bones of his prey.

Harald said, 'This is not your affair, Arsleif.'

But already Arsleif had grasped Haldor Snorreson by the wrists and, falling to the ground, had placed his right foot under him and pitched him over the middle table. The Icelander's head hit the kingpost of the hall with such a thump that it seemed the roof shook. But he got up and staggered back towards Arsleif, as though he thought nothing had happened.

Harald had no time to see any more, because at that moment Wulf Ospakson was on him, and trying to get his head fast under his thick right arm. But Harald had the measure of this, and as the arm began to close, slipped out of it and grasping the Icelander's wrist, helped the arm on its way round, jerking it behind Wulf's back so sharply that all men heard the man groan.

Then, leaping back a pace, Harald came in again and butted the Icelander in the ribs, while he was still nursing his injured arm. Wulf went down, with Harald on top of him, just as Arsleif ran to meet the staggering Haldor.

The men at the tables had already lost interest in such a short bout and were going back to their ale-cups. Arsleif swung out his leg and tripped the Icelander, then, as he fell, brought down his fist behind the neck. Haldor put his face in the straw and lay still, as though the journey from Iceland had tired him out.

As for Harald, he took a little longer over his part of the affair, but when he had finished, Wulf was sleeping as soundly as Haldor.

And when Arsleif and Harald had put on their shirts again and were slaking their thirst from the wrestling, Jaroslav leaned across and said, 'You will have made either two very good friends, or two bitter enemies. We shall not know which until they wake. As for my daughter, who caused this to happen, I leave her punishment to you, Harald. Say the word, and she shall be whipped like any kitchen-wench who misbehaves herself.'

Harald looked at Elizabeth over the top of his cup. She was staring at him white-faced and defiantly, as though she was daring him to say, 'Whip her!' Instead, he took a pull at the ale-cup and said in his loudest voice, 'Send her to play with her dolls, Cousin Jaroslav, for she is not yet clever enough to play with men.'

This was the first time that the lords of Novgorod had heard such words said of the King's daughter, and many of the older ones with the long beards, sucked in their breath at Haralds's daring.

But King Jaroslav laughed out loud and said, 'By Thor, Odin and Freya, you know how to touch her to the quick! One day, men will boast that Norway has the sharpest-tongued King and Queen in the Northland.'

In the gusty laughter about the board, Elizabeth rose hotly and went up the stone-steps to her bower. And when she got there she first gave her slave-girl's hair a good tugging; then she took a bone hair-comb and scratched it the length of a painted icon that had come up from Miklagard. Afterwards, she flung herself on her bed and kicked for a while, before sending the thrall to see how the Icelanders now fared, and to order them to her presence if they were fit to talk yet, since she had something of importance to ask them.

When all the feasting was over, and such men as could walk were making their way to the guest-houses, Arsleif said to Harald, 'Well, viking, this night we have made both friends and enemies. He who lives longest will see which are strongest.'

Harald nodded and said, smiling, 'As it was fated, so it turned out. No man can change the eagle's course by pointing up at him. As long as we are together, you and I, the whole world can come at us, for all I care.'

Arsleif patted Harald on the shoulder, but nevertheless, smiled a little thoughtfully as they went up the ladder to their beds.

Chapter Six

The Tax Gathering

Winter passed like a dream at Jaroslav's great court, for there was always feasting, or hunting, or listening to the blind bards singing battle-tales. At last, when the great plains outside the palace-stockade were stirring with life again, and the sun was growing bolder each day, Jaroslav sent for Harald and, in his secret audience-chamber where the stone walls were hung with thick brocades from Syria, he said, 'Cousin, some of the lords are beginning to say that I am spoiling you, keeping you here like a prized bull in the straw, when you should be out proving yourself and showing what you can do.'

Harald shrugged his shoulders and said, 'I am ready to go anywhere, and do anything, as long as there is profit in it, cousin.'

Jaroslav thought a while and said, 'Yes, you are a Northman; they always ask first what profit is to be gained. So I will tell you – in this venture, there may be profit for both of us, though yours may not be held in the hand for a man to see.'

Harald smiled and said, 'It is too early in the morning for riddles, lord. Come straight out with it, as the wolf comes from the wood at a lamb, all in a rush.'

King Jaroslav said grimly, 'There will be wolves enough in this undertaking. See that you are not the lamb! I want you to take a strong party of war-men and collect my spring taxes from the southern villages. Some of them have not been brought in for two years or more, and to keep up the feasting at this court I need good coin, or cattle on the hoof.'

Harald said, 'I will go alone with Arsleif to collect the taxes, cousin. You need not disturb the warriors from their feasting and hunting.'

But King Jaroslav shook his head and said, 'It would be easier to snatch a leg of lamb from a lion than to bring in my spring taxes, Harald. If you knew our Novgorod peasants better you would ask for twice the number of followers that I am able to give you.'

'As you please,' said Harald.

> '*Give me two, give me ten,*
> *I'll be there and back again!*'

When he had gone from the room, King Jaroslav sent for his priest and ordered him to light ten white candles a day in the chapel until further notice, and also to see that the prayer for safe-return of travellers was chanted at each sunrise and sunset.

The priest bowed his head and said, 'Dare I ask who is about to put himself in danger, voyaging, my lord?'

Jaroslav said, 'Oh, nobody, Master Priest. It is just a fancy I have. But see that it is done, all the same.'

The priest went away puzzled, and wishing he was back in Ireland, where the hundred kings had more sense.

As for Harald, on his way from Jaroslav's chamber, he met Princess Elizabeth up the stairs, trying to whistle like a blackbird. He said to her:

> '*A whistling woman and a crowing hen*
> *Are neither good for God nor men.*'

She screwed up her eyes and said:

> '*The dog that barks by the great wolf's lair*
> *Soon finds he's lost both hide and hair.*'

Harald said:

> '*This dog will keep his hair and hide*
> *And bring the wolf's pelt back besides.*'

Elizabeth laughed and said, 'You rhyme like a Khazar horse-trader! But, never mind, if you can bring back the King's taxes, I may agree to sit with you on the throne-chair in Norway – even though I hear the place is like a village-midden.'

Harald looked back over his shoulder and said, 'The time for that will be when you are asked.'

As he went on down the stairs, the girl whistled after him, this time like a mocking starling.

For days, men prepared to ride off under Harald's leadership, and soon they had horses laden with salt-meat and skins of ale, and spare fur-jackets, to see them through their journey.

The night before they set out, Arsleif Summerbird came to Harald and said, 'We have now thirty men who will come with a good heart, and the Baltic brothers are most anxious of all to follow you. If only we can keep their minds on the task before them, they should be useful fellows to have with us.'

Harald nodded and said, 'What of the two Icelanders, Wulf and Haldor? Are they coming with us?'

Arsleif frowned and said, 'They are nowhere to be seen.

They left the feast-hall last night, and their beds were un-slept in when the thrall-woman went to call them this morning.'

Harald laughed and said, 'We can well do without such quarrelsome hounds, father. We shall have enough to do, keeping the Baltic-men in order!'

And he spoke rightly enough, for less than a day south of Novgorod, the chieftains challenged all of the party who had black hair to fight them; and the next day, they challenged all men with grey eyes to wrestle them. On the third day they came and told Harald that, since he had not allowed these sports, the least he could do was to declare a holiday, so that they could all go hunting in a big forest they had come to.

But Harald only said, 'Keep your noses turned to the south, brothers, and when we reach the villages, there will be fighting and hunting enough to satisfy even you.'

As he was speaking, Arsleif stood behind him, examining the edge of his sword, as though he wanted to be sure that no rust had gathered on the blade. So the brothers said no more, and for a while rode peacefully with the others.

The first village they came to lay out in the open plain, with a narrow stream curling about it, and a half-rotten stockade of wood round it. The men and women stood in the middle of the square and pretended not to understand Harald's words, when he asked for the King's taxes. They shook their heads and pointed to their mouths, as though they were dumb. But when the Baltic brothers dug under the straw in their headman's hall and came back with five iron-bound coffers of silver coin, the villagers found their voices and called them thieves and robbers and murderers. Blutkind, the eldest brother, wanted to set fire to the village-granary, but Arsleif held his arms and told him to play fair; they had got the taxes, and more than the taxes, so these villagers should be left in peace now.

The next village lay four days away, and was very different. It nestled at the edge of a forest, and was built of pine-logs, so that it was hard to see where the forest ended and the village began. No smoke came from the chimney-holes, and no folk worked in the houses. Harald's men said the dark-shadowed place made them feel uneasy, as though it was inhabited only by woodland ghosts or trolls. Even Blutkind said that it would be wiser to pass this place by, and try to collect twice the amount of taxes from the next village on the list.

But Harald said firmly, 'The King has sent us here to gather his dues, and all who turn away from that task shall be named cowards, Blutkind.'

So Blutkind was the first to go into this place, to show his courage, but not even he could smell out any treasure there. Nor were there any cows, goats, or sheep which could be taken instead. Searching from house to house, Harald and Arsleif scratched their heads in puzzlement, for there were not even any pots and pans, meat-knives or bed-clothes; and the white ashes in the hearths were all stone-cold and damp.

Arsleif said at last, 'This is a dead village, son. The men and women have either gone into the forest and forgotten it, or something has come from the forest and eaten them up.'

Harald said, 'If so, it is strange there are no bones lying about, Arsleif Summerbird.'

Blutkind's next brother, Skol, said, 'If these folk do not need their village any longer, then we can burn it for them, can't we, Harald? There is nothing that puts more heart into weary travellers than a good blaze.'

Harald was just about to give them permission, so as to keep them quiet, when from behind the biggest hut came the rattle of wings, and a gaunt and bedraggled raven fluttered into the middle of the compound, where it landed and stood, looking from one man to another, with strange bright eyes.

Skol said, 'From this range, I could hit that bird with my spear.' But his brother, Blutkind, held his arm and said fiercely, 'It would be the last thing you ever did, brother. This is Odin's bird, and it does not stare at us fearlessly for nothing.'

All the men heard these words, and began to back away from the tattered bird, muttering. The raven made a step or two towards Skol, causing him to give ground, and then, with a harsh dry cry, suddenly turned and fluttered back to the forest. They heard its wings brushing the pine-boughs. Most men shuddered, as though a chill wind had suddenly blown on their backs.

That night, well away from the village, with fires burning on the plain, Arsleif said solemnly, 'I am not sure that this day has gone well for us, Harald. I had rather that bird had been a pigeon than a raven.'

Harald answered, 'Who are we to judge whether he came as friend or foe? Some men are too ready to think the worst when, by a little care, they could turn things to their own advantage. As for me, I shall consider the omen as being to our advantage, and from this time shall again take as my banner the black raven, and I shall call it *Landwaster*, because the land hereabouts is so ravaged and bare.'

Arsleif said, 'You can do as you please, son. But when we get to the next village, we may find out whose side that bird was on.'

It was three days before the tax-collectors reached the next village, and it was the strongest they had seen. Set on a high mound, it was surrounded by a thick rampart of turf and tree-stumps. The houses within the palisade were hunched and smoke-blackened, and on some of the roofs men sat, unafraid of showing themselves, laughing and drinking from skins, and waving axes and thick-shafted spears.

Arsleif said, 'These folk do not pretend to be dumb, or to hide in the forest. They want us to know they are at home.'

Blutkind said scornfully, 'We will show them what it is to taunt the King's collectors. We will burn down every other house in their market-place. That should bring them to their senses.'

As he said this, an arrow whistled out of the smoky air and stuck in Blutkind's calf. He gave a howl and fell on the ground, beating the turf with his clenched fists. His youngest brother, Ram, jumped on him and held him still, while Skol wrenched the arrow out and examined it. 'That was a shrewd blow,' he said, laughing, 'but you will get small hurt from it; the point is only of sharpened stick and is clean enough.'

Blutkind stopped shouting now and bound his leg with a strip of cloth torn from his cloak.

'All the same,' he grumbled at last, 'I am not as good as I was before it hit me. I shall have to hobble for a few days, I can feel. That arrow will cost these folk dearly; the taxes will be doubled, as far as I am concerned.'

Just then a whole flight of arrows whirred out of the air and knocked down a horse and three men. Harald saw that this time the shafts had done the most damage they could, and he called to his party to run back, out of range, so that they could decide how it would be best to attend to the matter.

Behind a line of stunted whinberry bushes, they sat and talked. 'That raven knew what he was about,' said Blutkind, hugging his leg. 'I now wish that I had let my brother, Skol, have his own way.'

Skol said, 'It would have mattered little. A great ox like

you would have met that shaft, bird or not, for as our father used to say, you have ever been too slow even to move inside out of the rain.'

Blutkind nodded simply and said, 'Aye, our father knew something. I wish he was here to talk to now; he would tell us what to do.'

Harald spoke sharply.

'That may be so, but I am your leader here, wise as your father was, Blutkind. And, since we have no bows and arrows, and would scorn to use them if we had, being sword-men and axe-men, our hope lies elsewhere. This we shall do: tonight, as twilight falls, we shall ring the village and come in at the blast of my horn, on all sides. In the dusk, their bowmen will be unsighted, and so we can climb the walls and teach them sense.'

All men nodded at this, save Arsleif, who said quietly, 'I do not hold with night-fighting, for in it many good men have met their end from a comrade's blade. But since you are set on it, Harald, I will not vote against it; but I will suggest that we each tie a white cloth about our heads so that we may know one another in the scuffle.'

All men nodded at this, too, and so they settled down to wait for dusk to fall.

It came faster than men expected; grey mists blew in over the rolling plain, as thick as fire-smoke, coming so low across the grass-tops that a man, standing up, looked like a bodiless head, or like one standing in the sea. And as this misty-murk came up, so the torches flared on poles in the village.

Harald said, 'They think to see all we shall do with these candles of theirs; but I hazard we shall be over the walls before they set eyes on us.'

Blutkind groaned and said, 'If the ache in my wounded

leg does not ease, I shall be over the hilltops to Troll-land, and no mistake.'

Harald clapped him on the back and said, 'What! You'll live for a hundred years, friend!'

Arsleif pulled Harald away then and whispered, 'You should never say a thing like that among these simple warrior-folk. It is like putting new shoes on the table – you tempt the gods to send you packing.'

Harald shrugged and set his horn to his lips. He paused and said, 'We should be ready now, ringing the village.' Then he blew a long blast, that seemed to set up swirls in the grey mist while it lasted. Then, here and there on the plain, the black shapes of the King's tax-collectors swept in towards the village-mound.

Arrows whined in the air, but Harald did not see any of his men who were taken by them. It was a steep scramble up the mound, but with Arsleif's hand in his back, Harald gained the top and then plunged at the turf-wall. Once on top, he saw that it was wide enough for a wagon to run along, and this disturbed him, for while a man was crossing the wall, he was a target for the arrows, lit as he was by the high flares. And here Harald saw at least six of his fellows go down, clutching throat or chest.

Then, with a high cry and a leap, he was down into the village street, with Arsleif beside him. Both had their swords out and sought an enemy. And such were not hard to find, for the place was thick with men. They stood shoulder to shoulder, about the houses, each armed with axe, or bill-hook, or javelin.

And foremost among them stood the Icelanders, Wulf Ospakson and Haldor Snorreson, dressed in their best gilded helmets and war-mail, and seeming to be much the chiefest men in the place.

Arsleif pulled Harald back a little and said, 'So, here are your enemies, lad. We gained little by beating them at the Yuletide wrestling after all.'

Harald said, 'An Icelander is a man, like any other. If you catch him right, on the neck, he will fall down.'

Blutkind, stumbling behind them and groaning with every step, called out, 'Then, for the love of Odin, catch them right, on the neck, for I am in a poor way now and I think that a reasonably fierce sparrow could outface me and put me to flight.'

The fight in the village did not last as long as one might have thought. Arsleif and Harald took on the Icelanders, and with luck came out of it, losing hardly more blood than a thimble would hold. And when the beaten Icelanders turned and escaped between the huts, the heart went out of the villagers. Some of them leapt the walls and ran over the misty plains; others set torches to their houses, and perished in the flames. All ways, it was a bloody gathering of taxes that year.

And when the dawn came, Harald saw that Blutkind and his two brothers were lying on the heap, among others, and that only Blutkind was still awake in the world.

Of his thirty men, Harald could count but nineteen who would shake an axe again; and these nineteen gathered round the white-faced Blutkind, for it seemed in his eyes that he might speak a death-verse.

And this is what he spoke:

'*I am going to the dark wood with my brothers.*
We have walked in the sunlight and have eaten good meat;
We have emptied many cups of ale and seen the fires burn.
We have had our share of giving and of taking knocks;
And though we dreamed of treasure, all we have gained
Is a good name along the Baltic, and a place in the hall

Of the King Jaroslav. May he remember us, and send
Coin to our mother who lives beside Kurland.
If I had the same life again, I would end it the same;
And I speak for my brothers, who do not wish to talk.'

When he had finished, his head sank down, and Harald put two silver pennies on his staring eyes to keep their lids shut.

'Well,' he said, when the burying had been done, and the just taxes collected, 'that is the end of one chapter; but it is not the end of the saga. For now it is in my mind to leave the King's tax-gathering for a while, and to follow the two Icelanders who have brought this fate upon us. Jaroslav can wait a little longer for his tax-money, and Elizabeth for her taming. I shall think better of myself in the future if I follow the Icelanders now and take the heads off their treacherous shoulders. Besides, it would be pleasant to see a little more of the world before we go back to Novgorod.'

Arsleif said gravely, 'Counting you and myself, we are twenty-one in number, Harald. From what I saw, the Icelanders had about the same number with them, so it would be man to man. And I, too, am not yet ready to return to palaces.'

Harald nodded and said, 'We owe Blutkind and his brothers some payment; so let us go and see what we can find in the world.'

Beyond the village there rose a grassy hill where black horses grazed proudly as though they owned the earth. And over that hill, Harald and the men saw a broad river which they did not even know was there. And far down that river, heading to the south, the keenest-eyed of the men said he saw a longship, going before the wind as though Odin blew in the sail.

Harald said, 'That is where the Icelanders are, then, friends. All we need is a ship to follow them in.'

One of the men swept his arms wide, to indicate the empty steppeland and the river. Then he said, 'Aye, that is all we need. Where shall we get it, Harald? Shall we go back to the village and build ourselves a ship from their stockade-timbers?'

Harald said, 'If I had that Elizabeth here now, I would teach her a thing or two for putting us in such a plight. But the day will come!'

The man said, 'I was talking about ships, not princesses, Harald. Where shall we find a ship?'

Arsleif answered this time, and said, 'First, let us go back over the hill and find ourselves horses. On their backs, we can forage further afield than on our weary feet.'

So that was what they did.

Chapter Seven

Over the Weirs

It was a week before they came to a straggling settlement by the riverside, where men were tarring a longship, knee-deep in mud, by the waterside. They were rough-looking fellows, all of them red-haired, and most of them squinting.

As Harald's men rode up to them, one of the ship-builders wiped his tarry hands on a piece of cloth and said, 'We have been getting this ship ready for you. When the Icelanders came through here, as though old Loki was at their heels, we made sure someone would be coming before long to buy a boat to follow them in. And so we got this out of the shed and here it is.'

Arsleif said dryly, 'How much would kind fellows like you ask for such a ship?'

The man wiped his face with the tarry cloth and said, 'Eight coffers of silver coin, and twenty-one horses exactly.'

Harald flared up and said, 'But that is all we have, and they belong to the King.'

The man smiled shut-eyed into the morning sun and said, 'And the ship is all we have, and it belongs to us.'

As they talked, other men came out of the various houses on the riverside, until Arsleif counted at least sixty of them, mostly carrying adzes and choppers in their hands, and all seeming to wait for a sign from their chief, the ship-builder.

Arsleif said to that man, 'You drive a hard bargain, fellow, but beggars cannot be choosers.'

The man grinned and nodded. 'Aye,' he said, 'we must take our chance when we can. We are not lords, like you men, who can just ride on to the plains and collect taxes when the mood takes you. We have to work hard and bargain briskly. Anyway, to show our good will, we shall stock the ship with food and voyage-ale, and, to top it all, if you bring the ship back in good order before the year is out, I will refund as many horses as you have men to ride on them. Is that a bargain?'

Harald punched one fist into the other in anger, but there was nothing to be gained by argument. So at last he agreed and they set course.

The ship they bought had already served many seasons and soon they found that it leaked at the after-end, for the caulking had dried out in the spring sun, and the hasty lick of tar which the villagers had given it was not enough to turn aside all water. So, while sixteen men rowed, eight a side, the others took turns at baling, often using their helmets for this task.

As for the rowers, they were soft-handed, being inland Lords of Novgorod and not shore-vikings, and after three days most of them would willingly have exchanged the ash-oar for the sword again. But Harald taunted them and said, 'What are raw hands and aching backs? The Blutkind brothers would be glad to sit where you are now, and would count it a good bargain. Besides, do not forget that, from the rocks and bushes beside the river, eyes may be watching us always, and it would go ill for the fame of the Novgorod Lords if word went round among the tribes that they cried like girls at the oars' kiss.'

After that, the men went at it with less complaint; but, all the same, it was a hard row and the wind from the plains now did little to push the ship along.

Sometimes, at night, the sharpest-eyed of the crew saw fires on high ground, along the river's course, well ahead, and this kept them going in the chase; though by day they never saw a sign of the ship they were pursuing.

Harald was as weary as his fellows at this, and at the wild and dreary land that spread on either side of them. He said to Arsleif, 'This is a lonely land. It must be the end of the world. These black woods, and grey rocks, and oceans of grassland with the mist over them, are terrible. Each day is the same, Arsleif. Can it never change? Will the sun never shine on us?'

Arsleif leaned against the gunwale and said, 'All men who seek the south must pass through this. And if you think this is the end of the world, you should try the desert between Zaragoza and Cartagena! There, not even the eagle can live. Have courage, lad, and I promise you that before we have passed the Weirs, you will see the sun. And when you have seen it, perhaps you will long for these mists again for, as the year passes on, heat strikes from the sky down there like a great hammer.'

And that was how it was. Within another week, as the summer unfolded, the sun came out from a cloudless blue sky and thrashed the rowers like thralls flailing barley after the harvest. Even the strongest of the Lords began to groan, and some of them fell off their seats gasping. Now Harald shortened the rowing-spells, and pulled into the river-bank more often when the sun was at its height.

He said, 'This way it will take longer to catch the Icelanders – but what profit would there be to come up with them when we are hardly strong enough to shake a willow-wand, much less a sword?'

Arsleif answered, 'The same sun beats on them, Harald. And when we do find them, we shall forget this rowing.'

Looking the length of the ship, no man would have thought that the sunburnt, half-naked wretches who rowed it were the Lords of Novgorod. By now, because they had eaten so much salt meat, and sat so much in the sun, most of them had sores on their bodies, and since their great rowing-thirst had used up all the voyage-ale, they were forced to drink from the river itself, and now many of them complained of stomach-pains.

Then, just when they thought life could not be more cruel, they came to the Weirs. This was a grim and rocky place, where the water suddenly rushed downwards among great boulders, its course twisting so much that no one could see where the river wound next.

Arsleif said, 'This is where we get calluses on the shoulders as well as on the hands, Harald. No man can take a ship along the river here. Instead, we must drag it ashore and build a wagon or sledge for it, to move it overland.'

When the men heard this, many of them fell forward and let their oars ride in the rowlocks with despair. But Arsleif laughed at them and said, 'Cheer up, lads, if you can play the ox for a week, you will come out into clear water, among the great plains and the rolling hills, with nothing then between you and Miklagard itself!'

One of the Lords, a grey-bearded man called Raskof, groaned, 'If I were back in my hall, with my feet under my own table, I would pay all the taxes to King Jaroslav, on behalf of the peasants, for a half-year.'

Harald said, 'We will remember that, Raskof, when we get back. Jaroslav will want to know where his eight coffers of silver coin have gone.'

But Raskof only groaned and turned his watery eyes away;

and Arsleif went to him and put his hand on the Lord's shoulder and said, 'Courage, man; once we are down on the plain again, the wind will change. I promise you, there will be no more rowing after that. The sail will belly out and whisk us along faster than a stallion can gallop.'

But none of the men believed him; they were too weary even to believe that they were still alive. On shore, it took them three days to build a rough sledge from the stunted hardwood trees that grew beside the river, for most of the work had to be done with swords and war-axes, which are not good tools for such labour, being shaped for other purposes. Yet they did it, and hoisted the leaking ship on to the sledge, and also cut down twelve saplings as rollers, to lay under the ship as they pulled. For ropes they sliced up their leather-jerkins and pieced the lengths together.

Arsleif laughed and said, 'Do not look so downtrodden, men! Who needs a leather coat in such a summer? And when we catch the Icelanders we will take their coats.'

Raskof said, 'If we ever see them again . . . I believe they have vanished into the air, Arsleif.'

Another Lord said, 'And if they haven't, then they will have used their own jackets for making ropes; so in the end we will go naked after all.'

Harald said, 'So much grumbling among such brave warmen! In Norway, even great kings will go unclothed, if only they may carry a good sword in their hands.'

Raskof answered, 'Aye, we have heard of your baresarks, but to us they are little better than madmen, though you call them kings.'

After that, there was no time for argument, and no breath for talking; the way down the Weirs was like the Labours of Hercules. A hundred times a day men fell, gasping, or the poorly-tied ropes broke. Once the ship itself, unsurely lashed to the sledge, heeled over and almost smashed itself against the rocks in a narrow gully. When this happened, it took a whole day to get it back on to the rollers; after which, the men fell to the ground and slept where they fell, their mouths open, their arms flung wide, as though begging for rest.

Harald, himself half-dead, smiled thinly through cracked lips at Arsleif and said, 'If the Icelanders could come upon us now, we should be easy meat for their axes.'

Arsleif nodded and said, 'It is at moments like these when a chieftain learns most about his war-men. Yet, when the time comes, I do not think we shall be dissatisfied with the brethren we have here. This voyage has welded them together, like the edges of a good sword. The blade will not come apart again, however hard the blows.'

Harald began to answer this, but even as his lips opened, his head fell forward and he was asleep. Arsleif caught him and let him down gently on to a bed of bracken, then covered him with his own tattered cloak, from which the bright colours had now sadly faded, because of the sun and water they had suffered.

Chapter Eight

Burnt Longship

All told, they were nine days on the Weirs, delayed by their weariness and the accidents that befell them; but one morning, just before midday, as they came over a rocky shelf, they all stopped and gazed in wonder at what lay before and below them. It was an enormous, rolling plain, that stretched as far as eye could see, green and brown and golden in the sunlight. And through it, winding gently, ran the broad river, shining like silver and smiling under the summer sun.

The Lords of Novgorod now forgot their bleeding hands and their raw shoulders, and, hugging one another, they danced about like madmen, laughing and shouting until the birds among the reeds and scrub-bushes took fright and fluttered alarmed into the blue sky.

Harald now declared a holiday, and the men lay about telling stories and chewing grass-stems and acting as though they were on a gentle hunting-trip. And the next day, when they were refreshed, they rolled the ship down a mild slope and were able to set it in clear water once more.

Another thing delighted them; by chance, because of the jolting which the timbers had had, the leak at the after-end was cured. Raskof declared that this was little short of a miracle and that, when they were all back in Novgorod, he would describe it to the Bishop there and get his opinion on the matter. It might be, he said, that their ship was a holy relic. Indeed, he thought, it might be that one timber of it had come from Holy Cross. If that was so, then they who sailed in such a ship were, in a sense, blessed.

Arsleif listened to all this, smiling quietly, and then said to Harald, 'I have heard Christians talk like this before; though I do not recall this Raskof ever praying to his God in the hard days we have come through.'

Harald frowned and said, 'Do not forget, friend, that I am a Christian, too.'

Arsleif nodded and smiled. 'But I cannot say that it has gone to your head like strong ale,' he said. 'A man would not know unless he was told.'

It was later that very day, when, swinging round a bend in the river, with the wind full in the sail, they came on such a surprise that even Arsleif stood like a man struck unawares with an axe.

A longship lay among the rocks and reeds on the shore, blackened with fire, and turned over so that it looked like the shell of a tortoise, its narrow keel uppermost. Round its landward side, three rough ramparts of turf and brushwood had been set up, behind which crouched two ragged men, clutching their rusted swords, more like scarecrows than warriors.

Raskof stood up and peered, then cried, 'We have them at last, Harald! We have them, by the White-Christ! Here are the Icelanders!'

Harald flung out the anchor-stone, his hands trembling, and most of the Lords of Novgorod snatched up weapons, like hounds in haste to run down their quarry.

But Arsleif held up his hand and cried, 'Wait! This is not what it seems.'

And as he spoke, the men behind the ramparts stood up and staggered towards the river, shielding their eyes from the bright sun. They came on towards the ship, as though careless of chance arrows, until they were standing in the water up to their waists. Harald saw indeed that they were Wulf Ospakson and Haldor Snorreson, though less like men than skeletons now. In a cracked voice, Wulf called out to them, 'Let vengeance rest a while, Sigurdson. Though we are not friends, let us not be enemies.'

Harald called back, 'We have come to settle a quarrel that started at the Yuletide feasting, and we will not be put off now, Icelander.'

Then Haldor Snorreson flung his arms wide and shouted, 'For the love of Odin, use what sense you have, Sigurdson. If there is a plague, do men carry on their quarrels while all drop dead about them?'

Raskof shouted out, 'I see no plague! What plague are you mumbling about, coward?'

But, even as he spoke, a bowshot beyond the farthest turf rampart, and coming up from an unseen dip in the grassland, three score of horsemen appeared, wearing high fur hats and sitting hunched in their sheepskin saddles, like creatures of another world. And almost as soon as the oarsmen saw them, the air was filled with the heavy twang of bowstrings, and through the blue sky short arrows flew, buzzing like hornets, angry when their nest is disturbed. Raskof, who was standing on the mast-stepping suddenly cried out, then clutched his neck and fell backwards, knocking over two other Lords. The gunwales near to where Harald stood with Arsleif suddenly sprouted, thick with shafts, as though strange feathered flowers grew there. Pieces of the mast splintered off and flew about like the white flakes of snow.

Arsleif dragged Harald down and said, 'Lie low, my son.

This is something no man could have dreamed of. The Patzinaks have moved northwards with their herds earlier than I expected.'

Harald struggled to free himself from Arsleif's grasp, for at least ten of the Novgorod Lords lay pierced and writhing, their bodies now unprotected by mail-shirt or horse-hide. But Arsleif forced him to the deck, and it was best so, for shower after shower of arrows came, leaving scarcely a foot of deck space untouched, and quivering as though they were alive, when they drove into the seasoned sun-dried oak.

Arsleif whispered in Harald's ear, 'Even if we cut the anchor rope, they would ride down the river bank and shoot us as we rowed. And, God save us, we have hardly enough men left to row a fishing-smack now. If there are six unhurt, we shall be lucky.'

By the time the arrow-showers had died away, Harald could have wept to see the toll they had taken. Of the Novgorod Lords, as Arsleif had said, only six still breathed, and they were clustered under the nearside gunwales, afraid to move a finger's length, they who had been great fighters.

At last, when the sun upon the deck made the oak as unbearable as an oven-top, Arsleif stole a quick glance above the rail and said, 'The Patzinaks have gone now. The Icelanders are crawling through the reeds, back to their fortress, and if we are wise, we shall leap overboard and do the same.'

So, in the heavy stillness of the afternoon, that is what they did, to come at last, wet and weary, into the shelter of the fire-charred longship on the river-shore.

And there Harald and his few sat down with the two Icelanders as though they had never quarrelled in their lives. And Haldor Snorreson said, 'We may have had our differences, Sigurdson, but we are both Northmen, you and I, when all is said, and we cannot let a little Yuletide difference

of opinion bring us to our deaths from Patzinak arrows.'

Arsleif nodded and said, 'If men would only think a while before they rush into blood-feuds and vengeances, the world would be a better place to do business in.'

Wulf said, 'We have been penned here for a week now, and as you see have lost all our comrades. We have buried them as the arrows have allowed us, under mounds by the riverside. Most of them died without complaining; but there was one, the fellow who hired us this ship, who wept enough for all the others, to lose his profit and his life.'

Harald said, 'Who was that, Icelander?'

Wulf said, 'A little round man called Krok. A Swede, to judge from his way of speaking, and a true rogue.'

Arsleif smiled gently and looked at Harald with narrowed eyes. 'Well,' he said, 'it seems his roguery has profited him little in the end. He now rests by a foreign river, under the reeds, and his ship lies burned by the water-side. What is there to drink, Icelander?'

He said this to keep Harald from brooding too much on the memory of old Earl Rognvald, for Arsleif knew that this strange encounter with crafty Krok would set the lad thinking again.

Haldor came forward with a pannikin of ale. It was bitter with age, but much better than the river water had been to drink.

'Take this,' he said, 'it is our only luck. We still had a great barrel of it left when the horse-archers drove us ashore and attacked us. Doubtless there will be enough of it to last us the short time that they will let us live. So drink as deeply as you choose.'

As the pannikin went round, Wulf said, 'These Patzinaks prefer to surprise their enemy in the middle of the plains, then they can circle them on their ponies and shoot them down at will. But we are fortunate in having the river at our backs; so they must come at us from one side only, and that gives us a little while longer to live. They are a stupid folk, taking them all in all. Each day they shoot off their stock of arrows at us, then spend the rest of the time making others, to use on the morrow.'

Harald said, 'Why do they not charge your ramparts and have done with it, Icelander?'

Haldor answered this and said, 'They have no taste for cold iron at close-quarters. Besides, we have found a way of keeping their ponies from jumping the turf-walls; we light reeds and brushwood on the ramparts when they look like charging, and that breaks the ponies' courage.'

Arsleif said gravely, 'Aye, but such tricks cannot last for ever. When more Patzinaks come up, and the plain is black with them, your cold iron and brushwood fires will be trodden under by ten thousand hooves.'

Wulf said, 'A man has to go sometime, Summerbird, and it is in my mind that this is the last voyage I shall make. But that does not mean I should stand like an ox and let the axe fall on my neck without complaining, does it?'

Haldor poured himself another cup of ale and said, 'It is in my head to run out with my sword, the next time they line up for their archery-practice, and to see how many I can knock off their horses. As the days have gone on, I have come to think less and less of myself. Indeed, it would be a good bargain to me at the moment if I made such a run, and some skald up in Iceland got to hear of it and made a song about me and my friend, Wulf Ospakson. We should be remembered as the two vikings who defended their longship out in the plains, along the road to Miklagard. And that would be better even than some kings get at their end.'

Wulf nodded and said, 'If my tale was told in the hall,

during the same feasting as King Olaf's tale was sung, I should think I had lived a profitable life. What about you, Sigurdson?'

Harald did not answer this question, for his eyes had suddenly become filled.

But Arsleif said, 'You all talk like fools. No song is worth a man's life. You Northfolk are too full of headstrong glory to see sense at times.'

After he had said this, there was silence for a while, and suddenly the sun sank down over the great plains, and the evening breeze began to blow through the grasslands with a noise like that of rushing water, or of a thousand ghosts whispering together in the dusk.

And when Harald had arranged for night-watches, the men who still remained rolled themselves up in the burned ship and did their best to get some sleep, though each one of them clutched sword or axe to his chest, ready to jump up and defend himself if the Patzinaks broke in through the rustling darkness.

Chapter Nine

Flight of the Summerbird

Now that night Harald had a strange dream, in which his half-brother Olaf stood before him, holding old Earl Rognvald by the hand. They were not dressed in war-gear, as he had last seen them, but in coloured clothes, as though they were going to a feast; and both of them were smiling. And Olaf stood above Harald in the dream and said gently, 'Not a sparrow falls from the nest but God knows, brother.' And as he said this, a great golden light shone as from behind Olaf, and seemed to cast his long shadow across the plains as far as Miklagard, and farther. This bright dream-light bathed both Olaf and Earl Rognvald, and for a while Harald was amazed at the brightness of it, and dared not speak. But at last he plucked up his courage in the dream and said, 'Brother, things are going hard here. They are as hard as it was that day at Stiklestad, when Swein came with the Bonders to take our land from us. Perhaps they are even harder, for the men we deal with here, at the burned boat, are not our own kith and kin, and do not speak the tongue we know.'

Then Earl Rognvald spoke and said, 'That day, Harald, up above Trondheim, we did a thing or two, you and I. It was not all sadness, lad. There is a joy in doing, for Northfolk.'

Then Olaf with the golden light about his head laughed and clapped the old Earl on the shoulder and said, 'I watched you two in the woods that day, hiding under the bush while Swein's clumsy fellows poked about with their spears. We all laughed, we Northmen up there, to see how you tricked them.'

Harald became impatient in his dream, though he did not dare to hinder old warriors in their battle-talk, but at last he asked again, 'What of us, here, in the burned ship, brother?'

And Olaf came out of his jesting and looked down at him carefully. Then, smiling gently and stroking his long golden beard, he said, 'It can take care of itself, brother. Things go by rule, and from where I stand now I see you have a way to travel.' Then he half-turned his head, as though he was looking into another country, and at last he whispered, 'There is a city they call York. And close by that city is a river they call the Derwent. And over that river there is a bridge that leads into a green meadow. Now, in that meadow there will fly a golden arrow that brings the last message. But not here, little brother. Not in a place where the great banner does not stand. No, not here.'

As he said these words, his voice faded away, and his brightness faded with it, until Harald could see only the faintest grey shape of the King and the Earl as he awoke inside the burned ship.

And there was Wulf Ospakson kneeling beside him and shaking him, his face pale and drawn.

'Harald,' he was saying, 'wake up, lad. Arsleif Summerbird has disappeared. He is nowhere to be seen, though Haldor and I have searched all places.'

Then Haldor himself kneeled beside Wulf and said, 'Either the Patzinaks have come and taken him in the night; or he has escaped along the river and has left us to our doom.'

Harald was angry at this, being wakened with such news, and said, 'The Summerbird would not fly away from the nest so thoughtlessly, Icelander, when there are other lesser birds to care for.'

The two looked at him strangely, but said nothing. Then they left him hurriedly to go back to the turf ramparts in case the enemy came again.

And at last Harald jumped up and joined them, with his sword in his hand, to lean against the heaped bank with all who were left. Each man was faint with hunger now, and as they all gazed over the swaying grassland, the heat of the sun caused mirages to rise, and the air to shimmer as though life moved in it.

Wulf broke the silence as the time wore on, and said, 'I have not felt so lost before. Now that Arsleif has gone, it seems our hope has gone. I cannot explain it, for I knew little about the man, except that he nearly broke Haldor's neck at Jaroslav's Yuletide feasting.'

Haldor said, 'My father told me of him, when I was a boy. The Summerbird has gone in and out of men's dreams, through the Northland, for generations. He is no ordinary man. At this moment, I would say that perhaps he is a dream that comes to men when they are in need.'

Harald was about to say that this was not true, and that Arsleif Summerbird was a real man of flesh and blood, a fur-trader chieftain who had, in his lifetime, travelled up from Spain and half-way round the world. But even as he thought of Arsleif's story, he too began to see how strange it was. He remembered how the wild horsemen on the plains outside Novgorod had known him, as though he was an old friend, and how the shorefolk in Estonia had known him at their first meeting. So he did not say that the Summerbird was a real man, after all, for as the sun beat down and the endless grasslands sighed in the heat, Harald was no longer sure of anything. Even the sword in his hand had suddenly lost weight, as though it did not exist save in the eye; and his fingers had lost their touch, as though he himself was slowly becoming a ghost.

Then, in the midst of this silent light-headed waiting, this gradual changing of values and natures, Harald's ears caught the sound of a deep slow rumbling, as though the earth of the great plains was stirring into life. He glanced about him and saw that the other men had also heard this noise, and were listening like hounds outside a fox's hole.

And at last, at first far off, then gradually coming closer, they all saw the Patzinaks, in hordes so great that they covered the grasslands, making them black with horses and fur-cloaks.

Wulf grasped his sword and shook it, as though to be sure that he still held it. Then he said, 'So, this is why they waited, so as to come in their thousands against us. Well, at least we can say this, that a handful of Northfolk are the match of a thousand Patzinaks!'

But Haldor, who was keener-sighted, suddenly said, 'They are coming at the slow march, not the charge, Wulf. And in their van, before the host, their High-King is riding un-armed.'

Then the Northfolk climbed up on to the turf ramparts to see the better, and they knew that what Haldor said was true. As the hordes came nearer and nearer, the waiting defenders saw that a small band of horsemen rode far before their great army.

And so, in utter silence, the enemy came on, until at last the foremost band, of a dozen riders, was little more than a long bowshot away. Then the whole host stopped and stood still under the sun, and the quietness was terrible to bear.

Wulf said, 'It is almost my wish that they should charge now and let us be rid of the waiting.'

But Harald said, 'Now Arsleif has gone, I care not which way the battle sways. In the night I was reminded of two friends I have lost; and this morning I awake to lose a third. How can the priests tell us that God is good, and life is good, if we lose our friends so easily? Life is nothing if there are not friends in it to share with.'

Haldor said, 'That is in my mind also, Sigurdson. Yet, we can say this, that in the short time we have been together behind this turf rampart and in the burned boat, we have learned friendship, though we began as enemies. That is something, surely?'

Harald smiled bitterly and said, 'Aye, that is something. For, as the women up in Orkney say, "Half a loaf is better than no bread at all."'

Then suddenly they stopped talking, because the foremost group of Patzinaks had come close and were bunched together at the side of their High-King and behind him. And, at the low mourning of a horn, these riders at side and back slowly hoisted up great icons, or stiff banners on poles, so that the High-King sat alone, enclosed on three sides by the immense paintings, as though he was in a coloured room of his palace, about to give an audience.

Wulf said, 'Those icons have been stolen from Miklagard. They are too splendid for these savages to have made, themselves.'

Haldor said, 'Maybe some rebel Bulgar-Captain has traded them to these folk, some time-expired Varanger who has robbed the Emperor's treasure-room, or his churches.'

But Harald was watching the Patzinak High-King, who was a little shrivelled monkey of a man, perched high on his sheepskin saddle, with a tall gold crown, shaped like the dome of a basilica, on his shaven parchment-yellow head.

At first, Harald did not understand the words the High-King was speaking, because of the sighing of the grasses and the wind, and because he spoke the Northern steppe-tongue so quaintly.

But after a while, the boy's ears became tuned to the old man's words, and he heard him say: 'The task is ended. The bargain is fulfilled. We have waited half a lifetime for the Summerbird to come to us, and now that he is within our tents, we ask no more. Go in peace, Northmen, and trouble us no longer. You shall have your lives, for we have the Summerbird, who has given himself up so that you shall go free. I have spoken.'

When Harald heard these words, his grief burst all bounds of reason and, giving a loud cry, he vaulted the turf rampart and, swinging *Whitefang* wildly in the air, rushed towards the icons, shouting, 'What are our lives, Patzinak dog, compared with that of Summerbird! Set him free, or never move from this place alive!'

He ran, lightfooted, his head full of the sun, baresark for the first time, laughing madly yet weeping as he raced across the ground.

For a while the High-King sat staring at him in curious wonder then, seeing that the youth would not halt in his head-long career until death overtook him, half-turned in the saddle and raised his right hand in signal to the warriors who clustered behind.

And all at once, the air was filled with the heavy drone of arrows. Their short shafts, plunged half their length into the earth, completely ringed Harald as a stockade rings a penned bull. And before him row upon row of arrows stood, like soldiers in perfect line, or like a great square sacred carpet on which no foot might tread, and all as thickly

placed as the spines upon a hedgehog's back.

Shocked into sense, Harald halted, then losing his balance fell among the arrows. And as he lay on their broken shafts, defeated and weeping, he seemed to hear a voice somewhere above him saying, 'Go back, Harald. Go back. There will be time enough to dare the arrows when the years lie heavier on your back. In peace now, go back!'

But whether it was the Summerbird's voice or Olaf's, Harald did not know. Then the Patzinak king smiled and bowed his head a little, so that the sun, suddenly glinting on the golden dome of his crown, struck full into Harald's eyes, blinding him for the moment, rendering him helpless on the ground.

And, as the other Northfolk stood still, amazed, on the ramparts, the great icons fluttered down, the troop turned about, opening a space to let their High-King ride through, and almost in a twinkling the whole great horde had swung round and was retreating, off among the shimmering grasslands, into the blinding haze made by the summer sun.

It was long before the sound of their slow hooves died away and the plains had ceased shuddering. And when all was silent again, Harald found himself kneeling among the arrows on the hot earth and weeping for the loss of Arsleif Summerbird, who had ransomed them with his own life.

At last, as the sun began to slide down the sky and the twilight began to move upwards like a faint dust on the horizon, Wulf Ospakson came and led him back to the ramparts, and said, 'We are too few to take your ship back up the Weirs now, Harald. Yet we must shift for ourselves, if we are to live at all. What do you say we do?'

Harald held up his head and looked about him. It would be madness, he knew, to strike out on foot across the great plains, for a man might starve among the grasslands, or die

of thirst. After a while he said, 'What lies down there, the way the river runs, Icelander?'

Haldor Snorreson said, 'The city of Kiev, and beyond that, the city of Miklagard, where the Great Emperor sits on a golden chair.'

Harald wiped the dust from his sword and pushed it carefully into the scabbard once again. Then he brushed the damp hair from his eyes and said, 'Then let us take the river-road south, the way the birds fly when summer is over. Perhaps Miklagard will be kinder to us than Novgorod was. Perhaps there is still something waiting for the last of the wanderbirds, the last of the vikings.'

And so they left the turf ramparts and the charred timbers, and walked through the sighing reeds to where the ship swung against the anchor-stone.

Epilogue

The sun was sliding from the sky and the dust was settling. King Harald of Norway had to blink and shake his head to persuade himself that this was not the sun and dust of the great plains above Kiev, but the sun and dust of England. A dozen times he brushed the sweat from his eyes and gazed above the milling throng of fighters towards the cool green Derwent river. Like a man coming out of a long sleep, he said to himself, 'No, that is not the Dnieper, not the place where we left the burned longship. It is just an English river after all, and I have been dreaming. Ah, I am getting old, to let my thoughts wander away so long in the midst of battle!'

There were many Englishmen who lay at his feet on the bruised turf, about *Landwaster*, who would not have said the King of Norway was too old: but now they could not speak.

Setting his broad back against the ash-pole, Harald called out to Styrkar, 'How is it going, Marshal? I cannot see for the crowds.'

Styrkar was in the middle of a knot of men, who were hacking and stabbing at him like wild beasts. His helmet was cracked down the middle, and of his mail-shirt only the right sleeve still clung to him. But he found time to answer,

'Tostig, our ally, is down. The English king put the axe to his brother's neck. But, from where I am, things seem to be going well enough.' Then, taking a deep breath, Styrkar flung away his shield and, grasping his axe with both hands, went at it afresh, clearing a new space round himself and sending the English back as though they were of no account. Each time the axe-edge bit, he said, 'This is for Ljot who held the bridge.' He said this more times than there are fingers on two hands, and never once did anyone answer him back.

Harald of Norway was not idle, either. If he had been a wood-cutter, you might have said he had done a week's felling in that one day by the Derwent, in spite of the heat and the thirsty dust. Not all of it sappy wood and alder, either; but hard-knurled oak mostly, that twisted and jarred along the blade-edge, until chopper and chopped alike felt need for resting.

But there is no resting for a warrior-man beset by enemy-hounds. Though he stand seven feet tall, there will always be some low-bellied cur to creep in and bite if he looks away but once, or blinks his eyes in the sun.

And a bite on the ankle can bring a giant down as surely as a thunder-knock on the head.

At such times, a man must keep up his swaying and his sword-flailing, holding his shield to left and right in time to the strokes that come, swinging his iron head backwards and forwards to miss stray blows. No man can hope to miss every knock. It is like running through a rain shower: some drops are bound to strike, however many others miss and fall to the ground. It is this way in a storm, or a battle, or in life itself. Even great gods bear wounds. The only man who bears no wounds has never lived: he is a dead man, although he breathes and smiles and puts bread to his mouth.

It is better for a man to stand upright like a tree and chance what storm may shower upon his shoulders: for, standing high, he may see across the stone hills, through the red rain, and glimpse the many-coloured rainbow of his dreams.

This did Harald of Norway, towards sunset, with the grass all snow-frothed and crimson-carpeted about him, and cattle in the yonder fields lowing to be milked.

By now, there were fewer men moving than had moved earlier; and *Landwaster's* silken edges were all torn and tattered by the wind's day-long biting. To strike blows and get blows by the hour is much like drinking horn after horn of ale. There is a drunkenness to it that separates the hand from the memory; and while the one goes about its task of hewing and heaving, the other will wander away along rivers and over seas that have been dried up half a lifetime.

King Harald sailed such seas, while his right and left hands guarded *Landwaster*. He saw himself standing between Wulf and Haldor, before the Emperor's peacock throne at Miklagard, taking the oath to serve him well and put an end to all His Serene Majesty's enemies. He saw himself and the Icelanders outwitting Saracens in Sicily; or standing guard over the stone-masons in Jerusalem, when they set up the new shrine to Jesus Christ there. He saw himself laughing in the sunlight and urging the oarsmen over the harbour-chain when, at last, he wished to come away from Miklagard, his fortune made.

'Oh,' he said to himself beside Derwent, 'but I have lived a good life, that I have!'

Best of all was coming back up the Dnieper to Kiev and taming wild Elizabeth and marrying her. It was a wedding to remember for ever, with the many maidens all in white and the candles blazing in the great church, and the choir-boys singing like angels before the golden altar. And old Jaroslav rubbing his ringed hands and smiling, as though he had got Thor for a son-in-law, at least.

Harald leaned against the ash-pole, breathing hard now, for he had done more than dream that afternoon. Aloud, he said, 'I have a good wife, my friends. And I have two sons, Magnus and Olaf. I have two daughters, also, Maria and Ingigerd. My wife and daughters wait for me on Orkney. My son, Olaf, waits for me on the Humber with all my ships. My other son, Magnus, sits on the throne chair in Trondheim, keeping it warm till I return.'

The English carles heard him say this and nodded, smiling at him as they drove in. One of them, a brisk axe-man from Ketelby near Lincoln, said, 'Then you have a good family, Hardrada. But I doubt if Prince Magnus can keep the throne warm for you, the time it will take you to sit on it again.'

'Oh, I don't know,' said Harald Hardrada, and swept the carle's head off his shoulders with one blow. For a moment he glanced at the body still standing with the axe held in its hands, then he said, 'Who is there for a king to talk to now? There get to be fewer good men in the world every hour, I do declare!'

There was an English carle named Edward of Saxondale, from near Nottingham. He lacked one arm and one eye, but there was no better dagger-man in the county. He stepped close to the Hardrada and said, 'Oh, take it not so hard, Norway. A man like you will always find someone to talk to.'

Harald swept out at him, but Edward Saxondale-carle was not there: he was inside the king's guard, almost breast to breast with him and the mail-links rubbing together harshly.

'Here I am, Hardrada,' he said gaily. 'And here is my dagger. Now, what were you saying?'

Hardrada was blowing like a winded stag, held at bay, but as he felt the knife-point searching his net-shirt, he said, 'I was mentioning that I had a good family, carle. And I will tell you in confidence, for I know you will not spread the news, that I named my little daughter Maria after a Greek princess I once knew in Miklagard. Oh, she was a darling girl, and if I had not been already betrothed, I might have stayed down there among the palm-trees and golden chalices, and have married her.'

Edward Saxondale-carle was about to answer with another jest when suddenly he lost all his breath, and never got it back again. Hardrada picked the dagger out of his mail-shirt and flung it over his shoulder.

For a time now the English stood away and let him be. One of them said aloud, 'It is a thousand pities you cannot be our king and sit in the West Minster, Hardrada. We should like it well.'

Harald smiled at him wearily and brushed the sweat from his streaming face. 'Aye,' he said, 'and so should I, friend. If I could only sit down now, I'd even rule you from a milking-stool. I am so tired!'

While he was saying this, a small man in a gilded helmet stood at the edge of the throng with a hacked axe in his right hand. His face was pale and serious and his watchful eyes missed nothing. Putting his hand into his pouch, he drew out an arrow-head tipped with gold, then, turning to an archer who stood behind him, he said quietly, 'Fit this to a straight shaft and use it, Edwin. You are well within range now.'

Another strange thing happened to King Harald that afternoon, just when the russet sun of September was falling behind the beech trees to the west. Peering through sweat and blood, he saw among the toiling men the great back of someone he seemed to know. This carle wore silver fox furs about his shoulders and a wolf's brush on his helmet-top. His other clothes were of many gay colours.

Harald gasped with the shock of this sight and called out, 'Why, Arsleif. Arsleif Summerbird! You old rogue, you!'

But the carle did not seem to hear, and went on hewing at the trade he was there for. King Harald forgot his own war-business for a moment and dragged open his mail hood so that his voice should not be muffled within the iron. It fell about him on either side, the buckles broken, leaving his face and throat bare.

'Hey, Arsleif!' he called. 'Must I speak to you twice?'

Suddenly he felt the ash-shaft of *Landwaster* strike him in the middle of the back almost as hard as a pole-axe. Then his legs gave under him and instead of looking down at men, he was forced to gaze upwards to see them. Even so, it was hard to distinguish their features, for a dark red cloud was floating before them now.

The man in the fox-furs and coloured clothes turned just then, and the king saw that he was not Arsleif after all, but a thin-faced youth with sandy eyelashes and a brown mole to the right side of his nose.

It was only then that Hardrada felt the sharp pain in his throat and heard the harsh bubbling of his breath. He tried to speak, but a great black wave smothered him and shook him so angrily that for a while he thought he was back on his longship, sailing the winter sea from the Vik down to the Kattegat.

And when that wave had passed, leaving his mouth full of its bitter salt, Hardrada opened his eyes again and saw men standing about him; not his own carles, but men who wore the Wessex Dragon on their over-shirts. They were all big men with solemn faces, most of them carrying the axe over their shoulders.

The king smiled up at them and would have greeted them if he could, for he knew they were royal house-carles and all brave men, with twenty battles on their backs. One of them standing closer to him than the others, a grey-haired man, held something in his red-stained hand, as though he treasured it. Hardrada saw the tears on this man's cheeks. With a great effort, he shifted up on to his elbow and stretched out his hand.

'Show it to me,' he said, in a voice that was not his own, but piped and whistled at the back of his throat like an old man's sound.

The grey-haired carle bent before the King of Norway and put the thing into his shaking hand. It was a gold-tipped arrow-head, its point now knocked aside and blunted: but it glinted with a strange fierce beauty in the sun's dying rays, though its edge was gone.

Hardrada rolled it between his long brown fingers, not feeling it any more and now scarcely seeing it. Yet he knew that the silent grave-faced men were listening to what words he might wish to speak in that great moment and so, though the effort cost him agony, he smiled and whispered, 'The man who made this knew his trade.'

From the sounds about him, Harald knew that his words had been well received, though most of the house-carles had had to bend forward to hear them. Then he lost interest in the arrow-head and cared little that it fell from his hand into the trampled grass.

Suddenly he wondered if *Landwaster* was still standing and, with a painful heave, he began to turn his head and body towards the hillock-top; but the grey-haired carle laid gentle hands on his shoulders and said, 'Do not trouble yourself any longer, sir. Your great banner is down. See, we have wrapped it about you. Put out your hand and I will guide it to feel the fine silk.'

King Harald's eyelids were very heavy now, but his ears

were open and he heard all the man said. For a moment or two he tried to smile, tried to say that the fine silken cloth would be spoiled, and that he would be indebted if these good Englishmen would roll him over on to a piece of stout sail-cloth instead.

But these words stayed in his head and would not come out of his mouth, for all his trying. And at length the pale-faced small man in the gilded helmet came forward between the house-carles and, kneeling, placed new-minted pennies on each of the Norse king's lids to keep them closed. The face on the coins was the face of the man who held them there.

When he rose and turned away, he said to a quiet monk who stood at the edge of the throng, 'Such a man merits gold coins.'

Then suddenly, almost savagely, he slapped the leather pouch at his side. It gave off but a thin jingle. He said, to no one, to the air or the birds, 'But there is little enough gold left in England now; he must make do with silver. He has lived rough; he will understand. The last of the vikings will understand.'

Afterwards, he left the twilit hill and went down towards the river Derwent where his own brother, Tostig, lay among the many who had gone voyaging that September day. As he stumbled over the turf, he felt inside his pouch once more to find two coins.

More Beaver Books

We hope you have enjoyed this Beaver Book. Here are some of the other titles:

A Knight and his Castle What it was like to live in a castle, by R. Ewart Oakeshott

The Twelve Labours of Hercules The adventures of the hero Hercules, beautifully retold by Robert Newman; illustrated superbly by Charles Keeping

Travel Quiz A brain-teasing quiz book for all the family on all aspects of travel by plane, train and car

My Favourite Animal Stories Sad, funny and exciting stories about all sorts of animals, chosen and introduced by Gerald Durrell

Who Knows? Twelve unsolved mysteries involving sudden death, mysterious disappearances and hidden treasure, by Jacynth Hope-Simpson

The Call of the Wild The epic story of Buck the great sledge dog in the frozen North, by Jack London

Ghost Horse Dramatic story about a legendary stallion in the American West, by Joseph E. Chipperfield

New Beavers are published every month and if you would like the *Beaver Bulletin* – which gives all the details – please send a stamped addressed envelope to:

Beaver Bulletin
The Hamlyn Group
Astronaut House
Feltham
Middlesex TW14 9AR

550983